TEARS OF JESUS

THE SECRET OF THE
CROSS IMMOLATION SYNDROME

Peter Chavier

Dedication

This book is dedicated to the heart of Jesus Christ, our Lord and Savior, out of love, devotion, and gratitude for his many sacrifices for our sakes—the large ones and the small ones, the known ones and the unknown ones, including and up to his final sacrifice on the cross and his work in our lives today.

About the Author

The author grew up in a Christian family, studying both Protestant and Catholic theology in Japan and in the USA.

A former Catholic seminarian holding a Masters of Divinity, he has written several novels with theological themes. His prize-winning book, "Tears of Mary", which received the first prize selected from 8442 books, was published in 2010 in Japan under a co-sponsorship of Intel Japan and Magazine House.

Contents

Prologue

April 16, 2007; Red Hook, New York, U.S. A.

"I'm not going shopping with you today. Is that O.K.?" asked David suddenly, who usually enjoyed going shopping. John Donoghue and his wife Mary always went shopping at a mall in the suburbs with their only son David on Saturday afternoons.

The parents found their son's request rather odd because they were accustomed to seeing him dash to their car with a list of games and snacks he wanted.

"He probably wants to stay home and play the computer game we bought for him," they thought, and they decided to go shopping themselves, leaving him at home.

They usually talked with each other each night after David fell asleep, but they were happy to be able to go out, just the two of them, as it had been a long time since they had had such a "date". They had a lively conversation in the car, talking about their son and their future. While they shopped, they had a good time reminiscing about the good old days when they were courting.

They bought groceries for the week and came back home after about three hours. They slowed the car down and opened the garage door, using the remote control as usual.

They looked satisfied and happy after their rare afternoon alone as a couple. It was David's birthday today. They were going to make his favorite—seafood pizza—and, of course, cake.

They made a bet whether David would come dashing to the car upon hearing it approach. Both of them bet he would, so it didn't really turn out to be a bet. However, it turned out that David didn't come out to meet them.

"He must be absorbed in playing the game," said Mary. John nodded, and they took out big packages from the car and began to walk. As they approached the front door of their house, they saw something unbelievable behind the garden plants. The big image of Jesus on the cross that normally stood in the garden had disappeared.

They found David standing with vacant eyes by the pedestal of the cross. An electric saw was thrown carelessly near his foot. There were remains of something burnt on the ground, and smoke was seeping out.

The happy and peaceful feeling they had been wrapped in disappeared in an instant.

They heedlessly dropped their packages and ran to David. Mary held his shoulders and stroked his head. She then checked to see if he was hurt. When she confirmed that he was unhurt, she hugged him so tightly, he almost couldn't breathe.

"What happened?" she asked.

"I did it," answered David, and then he wouldn't say anything further. John and Mary were stunned to see their son's attitude and what had happened. They were desperate to figure out what had really occurred.

The image of the cross which stood in their garden was a treasure of the Donoghue family, and they were proud of it. John's father, James Donoghue, had carved it fifty years ago, hoping to hand down his faith and love for Jesus Christ to his descendants. The Donoghues were known as one of the most devoted Christian families in their town. This image of Jesus on the cross was the symbol of all this. The Donoghue family saw it as a source of infinite protection, and they treasured it.

The wood shavings on his arm and clothes, the lighter and the half-burnt newspaper in his hand, the ashes on his fingers, were all telling signs that David himself had cut down the wooden image of Jesus on the cross and burned it and nobody else. John and Mary's hearts sank in shock and anger to know that their young son David had so wantonly destroyed their family treasure.

"I've told you many times how important this cross is. Have you forgotten? This is a symbol of our family; it has protected us all these years. What a terrible thing you have done!"

John was so angry and disappointed, he yelled at his son. David was normally very gentle and rarely made his parents angry or worried them. They could hardly believe that their son had done something so horrible and abnormal. But it was evident that David had done it and that it was a fact they had to face.

"Why did you do such a thing?" John kept asking David the same question over and over again, but David wouldn't answer. He was silent, his head down.

"Why don't you say something, David?" asked John impatiently, and he shook his son's shoulders.

David had never seen his father so angry, and he couldn't bear it. Finally, he began to talk.

"Jesus is suffering," he said in a forced whisper, his eyes fixed on the ground. A teardrop rolled down his cheek.

"Jesus is suffering? What does that have to do with sawing and burning the cross? Don't talk nonsense!"

John was so upset that he could hardly listen to what David was saying. Flustered by her husband's rage, Mary felt disoriented. She couldn't accept the reality of what David had done, and her heart was disturbed within her.

"You are already twelve years old and should know the difference between right and wrong," scolded John. "You should apologize and tell us the truth about why you did it, David."

John was almost pleading with David now, trying hard to calm his own anger. However, David didn't apologize or speak a word. He kept his head down.

Mary was now as frightened by her son's silence as she was by what he had done. She feared he had mentally and emotionally gone somewhere she could not reach.

"Is this the gentle David I know? What on earth has happened?"

Half an hour might have passed. Seeing their son unresponsive and unrepentant, the parents gave up asking.

"Let's clean up together later. Wait in your room for a while," John said, and he led David to his room.

Before he entered his room, David said, "It's not that I don't love Jesus. I adore him."

"Then why?" demanded his father.

David lapsed back into his terrible silence.

John and his wife went into the living room and began to discuss what they should do. They felt that David was either possessed or had gone insane. Mary couldn't stop crying from fear and grief. John was slightly mollified by what his son had said about loving Jesus, but he still did not understand how someone could claim to love someone and then engage in what appeared to be an act of sacrilege.

"I'm afraid we can't handle this alone," said John. "Let's consult Father Medowid."

Father Medowid was the head priest of the Catholic Church they always went to in their neighborhood, and David had a relationship of trust with him. Feeling helpless, the parents decided to consult the good father about this nightmarish incident.

CHAPTER 1
Crisis

An Impending Crisis in the Christian Church

A Secret Conference at the Vatican

One morning in early July 2007, Father Seiichi Yamamoto was walking hurriedly on the road which led him to Vatican City, located in the middle of Rome. He walked in a bright shower of sunshine,

How quickly time passes, Father Yamamoto thought as he recollected the days he had spent in Rome. He had just finished his three years of study there and was getting ready to return to Japan. He was heading for the Vatican on a bus from the church that had always looked after him. The scenery of Rome, which he could see from the bus window, was, as always, beautiful. He had been ordained as a Catholic priest in Japan at the age of twenty-eight. After working as a priest for four years, he was sent to the Gregorian University in Rome as an international student to obtain a degree in theology.

"I'll be thirty-seven next year," he said to himself, as though he couldn't believe he was reaching such an age.

Studying was his major work, but he also worked as a priest in a church some days of the week. It was basically volunteer work, but he would sometimes receive some money as a reward. He said Mass at a nearby convent every morning, said Masses and sermons on Saturdays and Sundays, heard the confessions of the faithful, and listened to their problems. He visited the sick and gave them Holy Communion. He sometimes helped offer Masses at weddings or funerals. The Second Kansai Parish Region of the Japanese Catholic Church, which he belonged to, supported him by paying his tuition and his daily expenses. His book expenses amounted to a considerable sum, so the reward from such work was a great help to him.

As he hurried along the road to St. Peter's Cathedral, he remembered a scene before Easter in one of his introductory theology classes.

"We still have some time before Easter, but let's celebrate the resurrection of Our Lord in our own languages!"

When the professor suggested this, the students all tried to be the first to write "Happy Easter!" on the blackboard in their own languages. The large blackboard was soon filled with languages from around the world. That was when Seiichi was able to feel that the Catholic Church was indeed a universal church, existing in every part of the world, just as its name said. There was a unity and harmony beyond every boundary and that seemed to be a model for an earthly Kingdom of God. The Vatican was not only the headquarters of the Catholic Church, which had about one billion believers all over the world, but it was the home of the hearts of all Catholic clergy and believers. Such were the feelings of Catholics, especially those who had studied, worked or traveled there for conferences or pilgrimages.

Father Yamamoto remained in Rome for a while after he finished his graduate program. He was heading to the Vatican because he had been called there for a top secret conference. This was his first assignment after he obtained his Ph.D. in theology.

He thought of refusing it at first, as he had a reservation for a trip to Europe with his friends before he returned to Japan, but he couldn't reject the invitation because Bishop Ryuzou Hayata, his direct supervisor in the Second Kansai Parish Region, had personally requested him to go via an international phone call. Of course, he was in Rome, but this convenience didn't seem to be the only reason the bishop wanted to give the assignment to him. From the tone of the bishop's voice, he could sense that the bishop trusted him. This made him feel good.

The conference was to take place in a room inside the building of the Congregation for the Doctrine of the Faith, which is located on the left side of St. Peter's Basilica in the Vatican. The Congregation for the Doctrine of the Faith is a department responsible for problems regarding the teaching of the Church on faith and morals. The notorious Inquisition refers to this congregation. It was called the Holy Office from 1542 until the Second Vatican Council (1962-1965), which brought a great reformation in the Catholic Church. In modern times, it doesn't have the negative image it did in the past, but there still are some people who are inquired of in the Office and who are excommunicated from the Church if they do not recant theories that have been judged to con-tradict Catholic teaching. That is why people did not wish to be involved with this Office.

Father Yamamoto was feeling sentimental about leaving Rome, but just seeing the sign "Congregation for the Doctrine of the Faith" brought him back to reality. He took his Roman collar, which he had taken off, out of his pocket inside his suit jacket and put it back around his neck. He entered the room where the conference was taking place, feeling slightly tense.

The number of participants at the conference was about two hundred in all. The conference began with an opening remark by Cardinal Hans Rahner, who was the Secretary of the Congregation of the Doctrine of the Faith as well as the Chairman of the Committee for "the Cross Immolation Syndrome", a sweeping new phenomenon.

"The reason why we have asked all of you to gather here today from countries all over the world is because, as we have notified you by letter in advance, we need to report to you on the series of incidents involving the cross that have occurred in various parts of the world during the last few years. We tentatively call it here 'the Cross Immolation Syndrome'. We need to discuss how to deal with this syndrome.

"Since this is a problem not only for the Catholic Church but for all the Christian churches, we have asked the World Council of Churches to send representatives from some of the major churches. Please feel free to raise any questions or express any opinions, but please also bear in mind that this is an occasion to ecumenically deal with 'the Cross Immolation Syndrome' and that it is not the place to have theological debates."

Cardinal Hans Rahner spoke in English. Rahner was an excelling scholar who had been called to Rome from Germany almost ten years ago. Initially, he taught at the Gregorian University, but later he was assigned to be Head of the Congregation for the Doctrine of Faith. He was just over sixty years old and had replied to the Holy Father that he had wanted to spend the rest of his life at a small church in the countryside, reading and writing. However, because of his excellent abilities, the Pope had insisted that he come to Rome.

In his youth, he was known for his reform-mindedness, but there was a rumor that he had become conservative after becoming the Head of the Congregation for the Doctrine of the Faith. His audience decided to wait and see.

A Threat to the Christian Church

"The Cross Immolation Syndrome has been reported in various parts of the world recently, and it has manifested itself in diverse ways. What is common among the people involved with this phenomenon is that they all have intense feelings of both love and anger toward the cross.

The number of cases is not large, and the cases are hardly known to the general public, yet there are enough of them to cause us concern. The name 'the Cross Immolation Syndrome' is a tentative name which a few of us responsible for this committee have discussed and chosen at this point. We can change it if there is a better name for it," Rahner continued, speaking slowly in a serene voice.

"It has traditionally been thought that any negative feelings toward the cross meant that there was something evil in that person or that the person was possessed by an evil spirit. Such a person is usually thought of as having committed serious sins, such as murder or adultery, and may be harmful to self or others.

Some patients of 'the Cross Immolation Syndrome' have burnt down the cross of a church or have destroyed some great Christian work of art. These acts can be considered crimes. But no atrocious criminal acts such as murder, violence, or sexual promiscuity have been reported in the people committing these acts. Indeed, many of the people are of exemplary virtue.

Therefore, this syndrome can be considered different from the previous possessions by the evil spirits. However, it has the potential to become a great threat to the entire Christian church.

"Why does the Christian church fear 'the Cross Immolation Syndrome' so much and consider it dangerous although it doesn't correlate with any atrocious crimes?" an Anglican Church priest raised a question.

"The Cross Immolation Syndrome has appeared in various parts of the world and the number of cases has been increasing. The problem is that the negative image of the cross in this syndrome may severely damage the holy and divine image of the cross, and this in turn may harm the image of the entire Christian church.

"We Christians believe that the redemption and the salvation of humankind were accomplished by the death and resurrection of Jesus Christ on the cross. Faith that Jesus who was crucified and died is indeed the Messiah (the Savior) whom mankind had been waiting for is the very essence of the Christian faith, although this may seem strange to those who are not Christian. That is why Christians have revered the cross as symbol of their faith, as something divine and holy, even sweet and to be adored. Therefore, the existence and the prevalence of 'the Cross Immolation Syndrome', which has the capability of greatly damaging the image of the cross, can become a great threat to the Christian church. There is no doubt that if we cannot find the cause and the way to prevent it from spreading, and if the number of patients continues to increase, the image of the Christian church could be damaged throughout the world," answered Rahner.

Then a French Calvinist priest lowered his glasses, looking into Cardinal Rahner's eyes.

He asked, "Are all the patients of the Cross Immolation Syndrome Christians? If so, which sect has the largest number of patients?"

"The patients of the Cross Immolation Syndrome are all baptized Christians. They are not restricted to certain sects. They have various backgrounds such as Catholic, Protestant, Orthodox, and Anglican."

The French Calvinist priest pursued his line of inquiry.

"Does this mean that the Cross Immolation Syndrome holds hostility towards the entire Christian church, and that its purpose is to attack it, and that it is caused by some evil forces possessing baptized Christians?"

"We cannot draw any clear statement from what has been reported so far, but that's possible," replied Cardinal Rahner.

Then a Nigerian Catholic bishop asked in a rough voice, shaking his big body.

"Does 'evil forces' refer only to some spiritual existence or can it refer to a certain nation or an organization on this earth?"

"Again, we can't say at this point. But this can be used as an anti-Christian propaganda by those of other religions who don't think that Jesus, who died on the cross, is the Messiah (the Christ), or it may be used by communists or other atheists."

"How many incidents or patients have there been?" an American Catholic bishop asked.

"Approximately two hundred incidents have been reported worldwide within the last few years since the first incident of the Cross Immolation Syndrome was reported in February 2002. If we include those that are still unconfirmed, the number would be doubled. If it continues to increase at this rate, the mass media will soon know about it, and it is only a matter of time before the general public makes a commotion about it. The Christian church must prevent this by all means, before it becomes public." Rahner was adamant.

The others couldn't help thinking that if what Cardinal Rahner was saying were true, then, indeed, the Christian church faced a very critical situation.

Rahner continued, "The cause of the disease is hardly known at this point. It is most mysterious. Therefore, we have no means to stop it from spreading. Under the present circumstances, no one can discern whether it is a work of some evil spirit or of an evil authority that has a foundation on this earth.

"That is why we have asked you to gather here. We thought if we informed you of this situation, we might obtain some new information or insights or get some good advice from you. Now, Cardinal Stewart will report to you in more detail."

A British Cardinal, William Stewart, who was held a position of responsibility in this committee, gave a detailed report. These are the major points he made:

The Cross Immolation Syndrome Spreading

February 2002; Munich, Germany

A thirty-three year old Polish architect, Janos Gago, born in the Netherlands, broke into the German national art museum, Alte Pinakothek, in Munich and painted out part of the cross in the famous painting *The Descent from the Cross* by Rembrandt. When the guard noticed what Gago was doing, it was too late. Most of the cross had already been painted out with white paint.

This incident reminded people of the destruction of Michelangelo's *Pietà* on May 21, 1972. That act was committed by Laszlo Toth, a Hungarian born in Australia.

On that day in 1972, many people attended Mass at St. Peter's Basilica, hoping to be blessed by Pope Paul VI. Laszlo Toth went into the crowd and waited for a chance to break through the guard, and then he attacked the *Pietà*.

"I am Jesus Christ!" he cried out many times and hit the statue with an iron hammer and broke the arms of Mary, who was sorrowfully holding her son Jesus, taken down from the cross. He also injured the nose and the eyebrows of Mary. However, he did not touch the image of Jesus himself.

Laszlo Toth was sentenced to nine years in prison. Mass media worldwide sensationalized the already shocking incident, categorizing it as an act of terrorism against great art and culture. Many newspapers used the eye-catching headline: "Jesus hits Mother Mary!"

Not only art lovers but people all over the world, particularly those of the Christian faith, were saddened and shocked by the incident. Day after day, the media reported about Catholics and art lovers who mourned the incident in tears.

The painting-out-the-cross incident by Janos Gago also greatly attracted the attention of the media. Since what was hurt this time was not Mother Mary but rather the cross, the very symbol of Christianity, the impact on the world was even greater. Because Gago also insisted, "I am Jesus Christ!" just as in the Laszlo Toth incident, newspapers, TV and the Internet headlined the news as "Jesus Christ Paints Out the Cross!"

However, the reason and motivation as to why Gago resorted to such violence still remained unknown. He was confined in a hospital in Munich because he had been repeating meaningless words ever since he was arrested. He was diagnosed with a mental disorder. He was later transferred to a psychiatric hospital in Amsterdam and was still under treatment.

As usual, the newspapers, TV, and the Internet were full of various speculations, but almost all of them were outlandish. In any case, the public in general seemed to be convinced that a mentally deranged person had destroyed a precious cultural inheritance."

As time passed, attention was diverted from the incident, and it came to be forgotten.

No one considered it a case of the Cross Immolation Syndrome. People took it as an isolated incident. However, the Committee could not help considering this incident to be one very important case of the Cross Immolation Syndrome. This was because in addition to this incident, there were seventy-eight cases similar to it in which the cross was painted out in various parts of the world.

Cardinal Stewart continued to report on other incidents, one by one. All these had escaped attracting great public attention because they all had occurred in small towns or villages, each in a different country, all involving artworks by almost unknown artists.

However, they all shared one essential thing in common. In all the cases, the cross was painted out or immolated in some way. The participants of the meeting were all shocked to hear this and to know that so many strange incidents were taking place.

The Burned Cross

December 2006; Lviv, Ukraine

Tatiana Schevchenko, an eight-year-old girl who belonged to the Greek Orthodox Church, took the historic flag of the church with the embroidery of a cross on it outside the church, set it on fire, and burned it.

Mihael Kuzunetsoff, a priest who accidentally saw her from his window, tried to stop her by yelling at her, but it was too late. The flag of the cross was almost all burned. There was no one else other than Tatiana in the church hall.

In addition to Tatiana's case, nearly seventy similar incidents had been reported. In every one of these cases, just as in the painting-out incidents, the reason why the people had burned the cross was unclear.

The Cross Syndrome Affects Children

February 2006; Rottweil, Baden-Wurttemberg

In the classrooms of elementary schools in this town, there is a cross on the wall.

A strange incident took place in a classroom of one of the elementary schools. Some pupils felt nausea during a class and vomited.

There is no lunch service in German elementary schools. Children either go home to have lunch or have a simple lunch at some small shop outside or inside the school. The school at first suspected some kind of food poisoning. Yet the results of tests performed by the Institute of Health and diagnoses by doctors revealed that it could not have been food poisoning.

What puzzled them more than anything else was that the children who vomited all said a strange thing: "I felt sick looking at the cross on the wall."

This incident of having physical symptoms while looking at a cross was not restricted to German elementary schools. Fifty-seven similar incidents took place at Christian churches and hospitals in other countries. In some cases, there were symptoms other than nausea, such as heartburn and breathing difficulties.

"The Committee for the Cross Immolation Syndrome recognized these cases as symptoms of the phenomenon they were studying.

Unlike the incidents in which the cross was burned or painted out, there were no aggressive attacks on the cross in these cases. The Committee judged that such a symptom might serve to damage the holy and precious image of the cross more than the incidents of burning or painting out of the cross.

In past history, the pain of sick people was eased and sometimes illnesses were healed when the patient looked up at the figure of Jesus suffering on the cross. It often helped patients reach some sort of catharsis in their difficulties. That is why Christian hospitals put up crosses where the patients can see them, both as symbols of faith and also for their healing effects.

However, the Committee members felt that symptoms such as nausea and heart pains challenged and denied the healing effects of Jesus' cross. The incidents reminded Committee members of evil spirits in occult movies or even vampires that feared the cross in old movies.

Some similar incidents were reported by some of the participants at the meeting and the audience was shocked at them. They also thought that what was reported at the meeting was a serious problem for the entire Christian church. Father Yamamoto thought so, too.

There wasn't much discussion because there wasn't much time left. The meeting ended with calls for another meeting for further discussion.

Is it a Warning from God?

The Image of Jesus that Wasn't Burned

The second meeting about the Cross Immolation Syndrome was held a month after the first one. Father Yamamoto did not return to Japan. He traveled in Europe by himself, visiting churches where his friends, whom he had studied with together in Rome, were working.

Because there wasn't much time between the meetings, it was rather difficult for the same members from the first meeting to gather again so soon again. One third of the original participants sent someone to represent them.

On this day, Cardinal Stewart reported on the incident of David Donoghue's burning of the cross, based on Father Medowid's report.

"There is a new development in what was reported in the previous report on the Cross Immolation Syndrome. I would like to hear your opinions about it later," Cardinal Stewart made as a preliminary remark, and he proceeded to present Father Mike Medowid's report in detail.

Father Mike Medowid found it difficult to understand why faithful David, who always devotedly came to church and even served as an altar boy, did such a strange thing as cut up the cross with an electric saw and burn it. The priest consulted David's parents and decided to talk alone with him.

"David, can you tell me why you burned the cross?" Father Medowid asked him in a kind voice.

David seemed to hesitate to answer him. David didn't seem any different from his usual self. He carried no air of having done anything wrong.

"David, I know how faithful and kind you are. I can't believe that you would burn a cross without any reason. There must be a meaning, isn't there? You have a reason, don't you? From what I have heard from your parents, they think that you are possessed by some kind of evil spirit. I can't believe that either. That is why I want to know the truth and remove your parents' misunderstanding about you and relieve them from their anxiety," said Father Medowid.

David nodded a little and finally said, "Father, there is really nothing more than what I have told my parents."

"That may be so. But your parents were shaken up by the fact that you burned the precious cross and may not have heard what you said or could not understand it, even if they heard it. So, can you tell me again what happened? I'm sorry that I have to make you tell the same things over and over."

Relieved that the priest wasn't mad at him like his parents were, David began to talk quietly to Father Mike.

"I think it was last Friday night. I was saying the prayers of the Stations of the Cross, kneeling in front of the cross. Then I suddenly felt the pain of Jesus suffering on the cross. I had never felt like that before. It's strange, isn't it? I felt so sad, and tears fell and wouldn't stop," said David. Tears were about to fall from his eyes now.

"Jesus is suffering?" Father Mike repeated David's words in a soft voice.

"I said the same thing to my parents. But my father said in an angry voice, 'Jesus is suffering! What does that have to do with burning the cross?'"

Actually, Father Mike wanted to ask the same question.

Pure and very sensitive children often sympathize with Jesus' suffering on the cross. It is nothing unusual or new. It is not abnormal at all. In some senses, it is natural. Father Mike rather thought that for children to feel such sympathy was a symbol of their purity and tenderness of heart.

Just as they learn and understand that Jesus had to be crucified, die, and resurrect for the forgiveness of sins and the salvation of humankind, their sympathy for Jesus would naturally transform into a feeling of gratitude for being forgiven and saved.

He had observed many children who changed in such a way. That is why Father Mike didn't see any problem in David experiencing the pain of Jesus who was crucified. But it puzzled him as to why David burned the cross. He wanted to ask him about it. Just then, Mrs. Wit, who was a house cook for Father Mike, hurried in with a message.

"Father, Mrs. Parker's family called and said that she had a stroke and was carried to St. Francis Hospital just now. She is in coma and unconscious. They want you to come to give the Anointment of the Sick as soon as possible."

"All right. Tell them that I'll come right now."

Father Mike hurriedly prepared to leave, and he said, "David, please talk to me more next week."

As the priest got into his car, Mrs. Wit cried out to him, "It's Room 325!"

"I've got it. Thank you. Please call David's house and ask his parents to come pick him up. Also, tell them that I'll call them tomorrow. See you, David," Father Mike said as he drove off in a hurry.

A Father is really busy, David thought and he waved goodbye to the priest, along with Mrs. Wit.

Because he had had to leave in the midst of talking with David, Father Medowid visited the Donoghues again on Wednesday of the following week. He asked them to show him where the burned cross had stood. He remembered that it was a cross made of fine wood. It was a wooden image of Jesus carved by a respected sculptor.

After a while, Father Medowid, who was bending down over the ground, said in a voice loud enough for John and Mary to hear: "Can it be possible?"

"What's the matter, Father?"

"Is this where John burned the cross?" asked Father, pointing at a cinder on the ground.

"Yes, but what does that have to do with anything?" John asked dubiously.

"If I remember correctly, the cross and the image of Jesus were made of different kinds of wood, weren't they? I wonder if different kinds of wood burn down to the same kind of cinder."

They did not understand what the Father was getting at.

"What do you mean?"

"Has David said that he burned both the cross and the image of Jesus?"

"We haven't heard him say so, but we assumed that he did. Are you saying that he only burned the cross and didn't burn the image of Jesus?"

"Well, I just thought perhaps that might be the case."

"If that's true, that's very good news. The cross can be made again right away, but the sculptor who carved that image of Jesus has already died, and it's not easy to find someone who can carve such an image. But why do you think that David only burned the cross and not the image of Jesus?"

"I don't know why, but when I looked at the ashes there, I suddenly remembered what David told me the other day. He said, 'I felt the pain and struggles of Jesus.' He said that he had said the same thing to you," said Father, smiling a little teasingly at them.

"Oh, we were both so upset at the time, we don't remember him saying that, although he might have."

"It occurred to me that if David felt that Jesus was suffering and sympathized with his pain, he may not have burned the image of Jesus, because he had nothing against Jesus—he was upset at the suffering on the cross. Please ask him again, gently, without scolding, if this is the case," instructed Father Mike, and he left without seeing David.

It was just as Father had said. David had only burned the cross and not the image of Jesus. The image was put in a room in the basement where he would often play alone. David had gently laid out a mat, and the image of Jesus without the cross was peacefully lying on it. David had dusted it and wiped it clean.

His family and Father Mike were surprised to hear that he had carried such a heavy thing all by himself, but their hearts were eased somewhat at seeing David's usual kindly self back. They believed that David had not gone mad or been possessed by an evil spirit. Still, they did not know why he had burned the cross.

"We re-examined the incidents of burning the cross or the flags of the crosses and the incidents of painting out the crosses based on this report by Father Medowid and found that there is something common among all of them. As with David's case, it became clear that only the cross was burned or painted out, and Jesus himself was not burned or touched with paint," said Cardinal Stewart. As he finished his report with this remark, the tension in the meeting room eased somewhat.

The Original Image of the Cross

"Now, let us hear your opinions," urged Cardinal Stewart.

The first person who raised his hand was a German Lutheran priest.

"In the last meeting, I thought that it was adequate to name the series of incidents over these years related to the cross of Jesus 'the Cross Immolation Syndrome.' However, after hearing today's report, I begin to feel that the negative name, 'the Cross Immolation Syndrome,' might not be adequate. David Donoghue, Tatiana Shevchenko, and Janos Gago burned or painted out only the cross and did not harm the image of Jesus himself. David even sympathizes with the sufferings of Jesus. I think we need to change the name of the syndrome to something more positive."

"Indeed, the patients of this syndrome don't seem to show dislike for Jesus himself. But since they are still expressing their dislike for the cross, I don't think we should change the name 'Cross Immolation Syndrome'," opposed a Dutch Catholic priest. Some others nodded as though in agreement.

Then an American Baptist clergyman made an unexpected remark.

"Can we possibly think that the series of incidents does not come from Satan or some evil force that opposes the Christian church? Can't we think that it rather comes from something good? Could it be, perhaps, a message from God?"

A Greek Orthodox priest pointed out a contradiction in this interpretation.

"Don't the acts of burning the crosses and the flags of the crosses, or painting out the crosses in holy pictures, which can be thought as crimes, contradict the idea that the syndrome comes from God?"

"We cannot assert that those acts were crimes in the eyes of God. Perhaps they are expressions of indignation over the execution of Jesus on the cross. Jesus himself turned over the booths running businesses in the synagogue in a violent manner, didn't he? That would have been considered a crime at the time, but it was an expression of heavenly indignation."

The American Baptist clergyman said, "Some of you may already know of this person, but I am going to speak to you about him, because remembering him, I think, is beneficial for reflecting on the Cross Immolation Syndrome. He is Peter of Bruys who promoted a reformation movement of abolishing crosses in the 12th century, claiming that adoration of the cross was idol worship.

"Many people agreed with his claim and followed him, but he ended up being burned to death as a heretic. The followers of Peter of Bruys not only destroyed crosses, but they considered worshipping the cross as the making and adoring of images.

"I would like to draw your attention to the fact that, although he is still considered a heretic in the Catholic Church, Peter of Bruys is respected as a martyr in our Baptist Church for standing up against the adoration of images with true faith.

"Indeed, some aspects of his deeds were extreme. But he sacrificed his life in order to oppose the trend in the Christian church at that time of worshipping the cross. The Baptist Church even wants the Catholic Church to admit that it was wrong to have him executed as a heretic and to have his honor restored.

"That may not be possible. Nevertheless, my opinion is that the series of incidents may perhaps be a criticism or a warning against idol worship of crosses prevalent not just within the Christian church but also in the world in general."

"Could you expound upon that?" urged Cardinal Stewart.

The American Baptist clergy continued: "As we see in the world today, the cross is used merely as a decoration or accessory by many people who do not know the meaning of its salvation or the faith behind it. God cannot be happy about such a trend."

As Cardinal Stewart listened to this, he thought that more explanation was needed.

"Indeed that may be true, but I don't think that alone could make God angry or make Him give us warnings. In any case, I thank you for your opinion. Now that we have had an opinion that it may be a criticism against idol worship of the cross, Professor Jurgen Balthazar, do you have any opinion on it, since you have researched for many years on the topic of the idol worship of crosses?"

Balthazar, who was a famous Protestant scholar in Germany, seemed a little perplexed at suddenly being asked for his opinion.

He said, "I'm not sure if this will help you or not, but the symbol of Christianity, the cross, is now an object of reverence for Christians, and it is something adorable and sweet for them. It is also favorably accepted by many people other than Christians. But, as you know, it was not so in the beginning.

"The cross was originally the cruelest of execution tools in the ancient nations. The image of the cross around 30 A.D., when Jesus was actually crucified and killed, was considerably different from the image Christians and modern people have, who use it for necklaces or other ornaments and have affectionate feelings toward it.

"In those days, the cross was an object of fear, and just thinking about it made people feel sick and disgusted. It was an image of cruelty. People responded to it the way we might respond to a gallows, to a stake at which someone was burned, to a guillotine, the electric chair, or a firing squad.

"When we consider that hanging came to be used as a means of execution because crucifixion was considered too cruel, we can understand that its image at the time was one that engendered intense negative emotions. That is why the early Christians did not use the cross as the symbol of the Christian Church. There is no cross on the walls of the catacombs or any other areas used by the early Christians to escape persecution in the Roman Empire.

"It is no longer possible for Christians today and people other than Christians who like the cross to have the same emotions regarding the cross that people would have had at the time of Jesus' actual execution."

Balthazar said all this without pausing for breath. He stopped now to drink a glass of water.

Then a Korean Catholic priest raised his hand.

"Then why and how did the cross become an object of reverence and become something beautiful and venerable to followers of Jesus?"

Balthazar cleared his throat, stroked his beard, and continued, "Well, I will answer that. For many people, it was ridiculous and impossible to accept Jesus who was crucified and died on the cross as the Savior of humankind. The core of the struggle in Christian history is, in a sense, to make people believe this, which at first seemed impossible. It meant the conversion of the image of the cross from the cruel cross, an instrument of execution, to the reverend, adorable, and beautiful cross through which Jesus proffers salvation.

"Christianity made great efforts to effect this conversion. The great success of their efforts can be seen in the fact that it is almost impossible for the modern people to remember the original image of the cross as an instrument of cruelty, humiliation, and execution.

"There were some miraculous tales and legends that greatly influenced people to accept the cross of Jesus as something to be respected. These legends regarding the cross, which were sometimes fortuitous locally and played into the hands of power, played a big role in deepening and spreading the reverence for the cross.

"People thought that the miracles and healing that came through the cross were possible because the cross was God's desire and because the cross brought about complete salvation. However, the background of

the cross was forgotten by people, and the image itself took on a life of
its own. It has been accepted and passed down as though it were a matter of fact."

"What are some of the examples of the stories and legends regarding
the cross?"

In response to this question raised by a Brazilian Catholic priest, Professor Balthazar continued.

"The typical examples are 'The Dream of Constantine' and 'The True
Cross'. They are in the so-called 'The Legend of the True Cross'.

"This legend is based on 'The Discovery of the True Cross' and 'The
Admiration of the True Cross', two chapters in the *Golden Legends* by
Jacobus de Voragine, Archbishop of Genoa, who lived from 1230 to
1298. It is a story of the wood of the cross on which Jesus was crucified
and died.

"It was about three centuries after Jesus was crucified and killed. The
night before the Battle at the Milvian Bridge, which is said to have determined the fate of the entire Roman Empire, Emperor Constantine had
a very impressive dream. An angel appeared in his dream and said, 'Raise
a flag with the cross on it in the battlefield'.

"Constantine accepted this as a divine message and won the victory
by raising a sign of the cross, and he became the new Roman Emperor.
This is the content of the so-called 'Dream of Constantine'. And in 313,
Constantine officially recognized Christianity."

The participants of the meeting were engrossed in what Professor Balthazar said.

"Constantine's mother, Helena, was a very devout Christian, and she
decided to go on a pilgrimage to Jerusalem to look for the very cross on
which Jesus was crucified. The only person that knew the whereabouts
of that cross was a man named Judah. Not willing to reveal where the
cross was, he was tortured and finally confessed where it was.

"However, there were three crosses, and Helena could not tell which
the real one was. So, she decided to put each cross over the body of a
young dead man. She found out that the third cross was the very 'true
cross', because it brought the young dead man back to life when she
raised it above his body."

"This is not historical fact, is it?" interrupted a French Calvinist cleric.

"No. It is, of course, a story based on faith, and it is doubtful whether
it is historically accurate. However, what is important here is not whether
it is a fact for us in modern times, but how the people at that time ac-

cepted it. What do you think they thought about it?" Balthazar asked the French Calvinist cleric.

"I think, of course, they believed it as a fact," answered the Calvinist cleric.

Hearing this reply, the professor stroked his beard with contentment.

"Indeed, they did. The people at that time believed those stories as historical facts. And even today, many Christians in general still believe them. They became bases for believing that the cross protects people from evil and brings them God's blessings and has the power of victory. And this indeed is the important historical fact which we cannot ignore.

"Soon, the cross was used in various places, such as a crest on the Imperial flag of the Roman Empire or on the flag of the Crusades. Also, people started to believe that the cross would protect them from evil and began making the sign of the cross as a custom.

"Further, as reverence and faith in the cross deepened, people did not overlook the value of 'The True Cross' as a holy relic of the cross on which Jesus was crucified, and it came to be understood as something very precious, that gives favors.

"It was natural for people to seriously think that possessing parts of 'The True Cross' would bring them God's blessing and prosperity. As a result, fragments of 'The True Cross' were sent or brought to various places. There were so many of them that Cyrill of Alexandria sarcastically remarked, 'If we gathered them all together, we could rebuild the whole of Jerusalem.' The number of the fragments was enormous. This realistically tells us how eager people were to have their prayers answered through the True Cross.

"St. John of Damascus encourages respect for the cross by saying, 'We must show great respect to Christ who offered a great sacrifice, and also to the cross which was used as a tool for this sacrifice. We worship the cross because it represents Christ. We do not worship the wooden piece of the cross. We worship Christ who is represented by the cross.'

"However, behind these words, we can read that there was a danger of being bound to have a favor-seeking faith in the wooden material of the cross, separate from Jesus himself, instead of admiring Lord Jesus who humbly allowed himself to die on the cross.

"Of course, as a background to the miraculous tales, there was a theoretical basis constructed by theologians. There was theological evidence behind them. But for the people in general, naturally, miracle tales were more convincing than theological significance, and this holds true in any age."

After hearing what Jurgen Balthazar said, everyone thought that the idea of the Baptist cleric, that these incidents of cross immolation might be God's warning against idol worship of the image of the cross, might not be so far off.

The meeting continued, and sub-committee meetings were also held to discuss reports from various regions. However, nothing was resolved regarding the Cross Immolation Syndrome, even after two days of discussion. Furthermore, the problem seemed to have become more complicated the more information that came forward. Since it was urgent to solve the problem, the meeting was extended for another day.

Also in Japan

The meeting resumed the next day with Cardinal Stewart making opening remarks again. A Korean Catholic priest gave an opinion from a perspective different from Professor Balthazar's, reviewing what had taken place up to that point.

"We learned much from Dr. Balthazar. He taught us that the original cruel image of the cross was converted into an adorable and sweet image, and people in general accepted the miracle tales and folklore as though they were historical facts, which played a big role in making that conversion. Also, it is indeed important to be careful about the danger of reverence for the cross if it's linked with elements of idol worship and favor-seeking beliefs.   "However, in this series of incidents, there doesn't seem to be any direct connection between the burning or painting out of the crosses and the warning against idol worship. Rather, what seems more relevant to their motives and purposes is what David Donoghue said when he expressed his sympathy for Jesus' pain."

Balthazar said, "Indeed, I agree with you, but is it clear that David really sympathized with Jesus' pain?"

"Since we have no information other than what he is reported to have said, we can only assume possibilities based on what we have, even if they are suppositions," answered the Korean priest, with a hint of impatience.

Then Hans Rahner, the chairperson, spoke.

"Although we are in the middle of a discussion, we have just obtained a piece of important information that seems relevant. I'm going to report it to you now."

A moment before, a priest had entered the conference room and had given what looked like a document to Cardinal Rahner. The participants noticed that after looking at it briefly, Cardinal Rahner had consulted with Cardinal Stewart.

Cardinal Rahner continued, "It is a report from the Japanese Catholic Church regarding a Sister."

The people in the room stirred, and everyone looked at Father Yamamoto. Father Yamamoto felt as if he were being hit by a thunderbolt. Until this moment, Father Yamamoto had been thinking that the Cross Immolation Syndrome had little to do with him or the Japanese Catholic Church. He wasn't exactly indifferent to what had been discussed, but he had been attending the meeting more as an observer than as an active participant.

He had been making light of the issue, thinking, "This problem is related to the cross which is the symbol of Christianity. It isn't very important for the Japanese Christian Church because only one percent of the total population of Japan is Christian, even combining all the major sects."

That's why he was even sleepy today, in addition to having read a book until late last night. But he became wide awake after hearing what Cardinal Rahner said. He realized that everyone was looking at him, which indicated that now the Japanese Church and he were the focal points of attention.

"We think that the Japanese Sister may become a valuable source of information about the deeper causes of the Cross Immolation Syndrome, which we were able to discuss before based only on assumptions."

These remarks made by Cardinal Rahner caused a stir of excitement among all the persons present because they were taken aback that it had happened to a Sister and hopeful that they might be on the verge of finding a clue to solving the knotty problem of the Cross Immolation Syndrome. They were surprised and interested to hear that a Catholic Sister in Japan, a country which is not Christian, might have a piece of the puzzle.

Cardinal Rahner continued, "The Japanese Sister also feels nausea seeing the cross. It is interesting that although the other people with similar symptoms have never said anything about the cause of such symptoms, this Sister may be able to provide some hints."

"Has she said anything about the reason for the nausea which she feels seeing a cross?" Father Yamamoto spoke for the first time at the meeting.

"She claims that she has received a revelation from Jesus. Of course, we have to investigate thoroughly whether the revelation came from Jesus himself or not. Nevertheless, if we can know in detail about what she claims is a revelation from Jesus, we may be able to find the reason why she feels nausea or has heartache when looking at a cross. We also may be able to find out the cause of the other cases."

After some questions were raised following this comment by Cardinal Rahner, a Korean Catholic priest raised the last question.

"What kind of revelation does she claim to have received?"

"We do not yet know clearly in detail about it, and we have to look into it thoroughly. In any case, there is no point in further discussion based on assumptions. We are going to end this conference here, and we will have Father Seiichi Yamamoto, a representative from the Japanese Catholic Church, investigate the claims of this Japanese Sister which he will report upon at our next meeting. Do you agree with this?" asked Rahner.

No one disagreed, and the proposal was accepted.

However, Father Yamamoto thought, *Oh, this is troublesome. If I had known in advance something like this was going to happen, I wouldn't have attended this meeting.* He felt regret. But it was, of course, impossible to refuse the assignment.

The meeting closed and Cardinal Rahner and Cardinal Stewart called Father Yamamoto to their sides to make arrangements. Father Yamamoto put the documents and notebooks they gave him into his bag and left the meeting with a heavy heart.

Three days later, Father Yamamoto was on his way back to Japan for the first time in four years. It was a few months later than he had originally planned. On the plane, he let out a sigh.

He had learned much from studying in Rome. Of course, he had acquired much academic knowledge. He also had considerable knowledge about the present situation the Catholic Church was facing, information he would not have been privy to in Japan.

From his time in Rome, now he understood how enormous the Catholic Church was and what great influence it had in the world. He had also become friends with many priests from all over the world. However, at the same time, he saw more problems in the Church than he had ever imagined while in Japan.

There were a number of serious problems in the Catholic Church, such as its relationship with other Christian sects and various other religions, the sexual crimes committed by clerics, the problems of secularization, deterioration, and power struggles within the Christian church.

When he was in Japan, he perhaps had idealized the Vatican and the Catholic Church worldwide too much. He had lost some illusions. He came to know the problems within the Catholic Church, and it was painful to accept them. Yet Father Yamamoto felt that being able to see the reality was a great blessing. There were many difficult things that went on during the four years he was in Rome, but after all, these years were full of grace.

The plane took off from the Leonardo da Vinci Airport and headed for Kansai International Airport, flying over the blue and radiant Mediterranean Sea. Father Yamamoto was still tired from the meeting, and he was sleepy. He tried to sleep, but he couldn't. The joy of being able to work again as a priest in Japan and the big mission of investigating the Japanese Sister who experienced the Cross Immolation Syndrome both uplifted and burdened his spirit. All these and others crossed his mind as he began to reflect on the steps that had led him to become a priest.

CHAPTER 2
The Origin

The Search of the Heart

A Gamble

April 1970; Kyoto, Japan

Father Yamamoto's father was named Chuichi, and his mother was Fusako. Fusako's mother, Sato, was a devout believer of Tenriism. She inherited her faith from her mother. Sato would get up at four in the morning, pray, and practice cold water ablutions with the water from the pond in the yard. In winter time, the surface water of the pond froze. She would break the ice of the pond and pour the water beneath it upon herself. After breakfast, she would go out preaching to her neighbors. If a poor person came to beg, she would give anything she had. Once Fusako saw her mother pull out her golden tooth and give it to a beggar when she had nothing else to give. His mother told Seiichi later that she always clearly remembered that incident. Fusako herself did not have faith in Tenriism. Sato, in spite of her own devotion, believed that each person had to find his or her own faith and thus she never forced her children to share her faith. She did not oppose Fusako when she insisted on going to a Protestant high school for girls. She believed that every religion had its good points. Later, Fusako married Chuichi and accepted his religion and was baptized as a Catholic. However, their marriage was not easy. When they met and were attracted to each other and began to consider getting married, Chuichi was diagnosed with stomach cancer. Chuichi thought of giving up the marriage. He thought that if he really loved Fusako, he should give her up. But he could not give her up. Every time he tried to give her up, he heard a voice from somewhere in his heart that said, "You should not give her up." And he struggled even more. "Aren't you saying so because you just don't want to let her go?"

Chuichi asked himself this many times. He never had an answer, but he couldn't possibly think it was an unconscious justification of his selfish love. After struggling for a long time, he gambled on the voice that said, "You should not give her up." He didn't know where it came from or whose voice it was, but he chose to marry Fusako. But what kind of parents would allow their dear daughter to marry a man who might die soon after the ceremony?   On the day Chuichi was coming to see Fusako's parents, Sato waited for him, strongly determined to reject Chuichi's proposal to marry Fusako. On behalf of her husband, who had been ill in bed for a long period of time, Sato had to take on the heavy responsibility of telling this to Chuichi, and she suffered on her daughter's behalf, knowing, how much Fusako loved Chuichi.

"I'll be a devil for my daughter's sake," she said to herself many times in her mind as she waited for Chuichi,Chuichi came inside Sato's house to greet her, sat on the floor, bowed, and then raised his face. When Sato saw his eyes, her devil's heart died within her. The moment she saw the pure, clear eyes of Chuichi appealing for permission to marry Fusako, she was suddenly captured by a thought that came from deep within herself: *I'll gamble on the clearness of this young man's eyes.*

Sato stared at them as the couple rejoiced over being given permission to marry. She had mixed feelings. She was oddly moved in her heart; at the same time she felt anxiety.

What Sato did was beyond common sense or any logic. It was indeed a gamble. But as she saw Chuichi miraculously recover his health after life or death surgery and create a happy family, she was able to admit that she had made the right gamble. She truly thanked God. Seiichi remembered how he was moved in his heart to hear this from his father and grandmother when he was in elementary school. *If my father had not believed the voice he heard in his heart and had not determined to get married, or if my grandmother had not accepted my parents' marriage, I wouldn't exist.*

When Seiichi thought of it, he couldn't help feeling the existence of a power beyond the abilities of human beings, a power he had felt even as a child.

Late Cherry Blossoms

It was his father, Chuichi, who brought Christianity into his family.

It was in the hospital two days before his cancer surgery that Chuichi met Father Minamida, who exerted a great influence over Chuichi's life.

Until he found out that he had cancer, Chuichi had never really thought death had anything to do with him. However, since then, death had followed him about, and his fear of death deepened more and more as the day of the surgery approached.

One afternoon during the visiting hours, Father Minamida came to visit a Catholic patient named Arai who was in the same room as Chuichi. Arai had just reached age fifty and had liver cancer at the terminal stage, and his doctor couldn't do anything about it. All he could do was to wait for the death that was approaching.

Father Minamida talked intimately with Arai and put a piece of cloth that looked like a surplice around his neck. He hummed something and began performing a ritual. Later, Chuichi learned that it was a sacrament called the "Anointing of the Sick".

Chuichi's was about to have his surgery and he couldn't be indifferent to Arai, who had terminal cancer. He was concerned about Arai's attitude and facial expressions and kept his eyes on him. After Arai had the "Anointing of the Sick", however, there was a big change in his facial expression. He had seemed anxious before the sacrament, but now he looked very calm. Chuichi was deeply moved to see the striking change. He wanted to ask Arai the reason for the change, but after Father Minamida left, Arai closed his eyes and lost consciousness. Chuichi heard that Arai was moved to the intensive care unit and had not regained consciousness.

Chuichi was shocked. But as he remembered Arai's calm expression, somehow it calmed Chuichi's own anxiety and fear. He regained some peace and hope before he himself underwent surgery.

The surgery was successful. When he was able to come out of the intensive care unit, he found that Arai had already departed. He thought that the way one meets another person was mysterious in life.

Chuichi made a good recovery from the surgery and was released from the hospital earlier than was expected and went back to work. Even after he started to work again, he kept thinking about Arai's facial expression. He wanted to know why Arai, who was facing death, could have such a calm expression. This caused him to visit the church where Father Minamida was, and he began studying Christian teachings of his own will.

The words of Jesus which Father Minamida told him filtered into his heart. Soon Chuichi was baptized and started a new life as a Christian, filled with hope. Later, Fusako and Seiichi were also baptized, and they had a bright and happy life.

However, when Seiichi had just turned a year old, they faced a crisis again. Chuichi might have worked too hard for his company. At the health examination at work, his chest X-ray showed something abnormal in his right lung, and he had to be hospitalized.

Fusako was carrying her second child then. When she heard the awful news, she was at a loss as to what she would do if something happened to Chuichi.

From the first day in the hospital, Chuichi had to undergo many medical examinations. Every time he had a test, he keenly sensed from the unspoken attitudes of doctors and nurses that his condition was quite serious. He felt indescribably fearful when he thought he might have cancer again. He had a strong premonition that, if he did, it was hopeless this time.

It was his third day in the hospital. He finished his examination in the morning and was lying on his bed. Cherry blossoms were in full bloom outside in the warm spring sunlight. He was looking outside the window, but his vacant eyes were wandering about without focusing. Every time there was a breeze, the cherry blossom petals flew in the air and the falling petals overlapped in his mind with himself, who might die soon, and his heart was filled with sorrow.

As a final blow, his doctor declared to him that afternoon that the results of the examinations revealed that he had lung cancer. In those days, medicine was not as advanced as it is today. Being told that one had cancer was equivalent to a death sentence. Chuichi, who was Christian and the head of his family, had asked his doctor to inform him of the truth. His doctor had confirmed this with his wife Fusako, and she agreed to it and had accepted his will to know what was what. But when it was actually revealed to him, it was more shocking than he had ever imagined. The doctor did not guarantee the success of the surgery because of the seriousness of his condition. He looked sorry and advised Chuichi to be prepared for the worst.

When Chuichi thought of leaving behind his wife Fusako, whom he had just married a few short years ago, and the very young Seiichi, as well as the child in Fusako's womb, he was full of regret at his cruel fate.

The day of the surgery fell on the Good Friday of that year, the day Jesus was crucified. One of the patients in his room sympathized with him when he found out that his surgery was going to be on the day considered most ominous in Christianity, saying "The God of Christianity is cruel." However, when Chuichi heard that his surgery was going to be on Good Friday, he somehow felt a streak of light and hope coming into his heart.

There was not much time left before the surgery. Chuichi tried to prepare himself and write a will just in case, but it was very difficult. He took up his pen and then put it down many times. When he thought about the family he might have to leave behind, he was perplexed as to what he should write.

Why does God make me suffer like this? he wondered. Chuichi felt that the days he had spent studying Christianity, believing it and making efforts to follow it were all useless.

One day, he confessed his feelings to Father Minamida. Father Minamida listened to him without saying a word and with tearful eyes.

Just before leaving, he said simply, "When I think of you, even I feel pained, bitter, and sorrowful. Jesus must know your struggles even more. He is feeling pain and is sad."

These words of the priest penetrated deeply into Chuichi's heart. After that he began to think that he should live according to Jesus' teachings even and especially in midst of the hardship he was facing.

At the peak of his struggles on the cross, Jesus forgave his enemies, who were about to kill him. In a situation in which God abandoned him, Jesus believed in God and entrusted himself to Him.

Although Jesus was sinless, he was persecuted, cursed, betrayed, whipped, crucified, and killed.

In comparison to mine, thought Chuichi, *how much greater were the struggles of Jesus? Why did Jesus have to go such a way? How did Jesus really feel on the cross?*

When he thought thus, Chuichi felt Jesus' pain and felt so sorry for Jesus that he couldn't stop crying.

Strangely, as soon as he cried thinking about Jesus' pain and struggles, forgetting his own, Chuichi's pain eased. Gradually, serenity filled his heart.

The surgery took longer than was originally expected, and his right lung was completely removed. He was unconscious after the surgery. His condition was serious. He hovered between life and death. His parents and his wife Fusako began to contact his relatives and friends to tell them to prepare for the worst. While he was unconscious, Chuichi had a strange dream.

In his dream, he met Jesus. Jesus was in a light. He was so bright that Chuichi couldn't see his face or figure clearly.

But he heard a voice which said, "If you really believe in me, you will be healed. Search for my heart and feelings, and I will be with you and your family. My time is approaching; it is extremely close. Keep a pure heart and be prepared."

"Lord, I believe you," answered Chuichi, and Jesus quietly disappeared.

And then, a moment later, he thought he heard a voice, a familiar voice. It was his doctor's voice.

"It seems you have come out of the most critical stage. We still have to be careful, but you are all right now."

Chuichi miraculously regained consciousness Easter Sunday morning.

"Was that a mere dream?" he wondered, feeling his entire body enveloped in the warmth of Jesus' love. He had gone through the surgery knowing that he might die, and he had been ready to die. He could not believe that he was still alive. The late cherry blossoms he could see from the windows were beginning to fall. It was as though they had waited to fall until they saw that Chuichi's surgery was successful. The petals of the cherry blossoms were blowing in a gentle breeze, with the blue sky in the background, and they all shone in his eyes.

He saw the faces of his family, friends, Father Minamida, and his doctor beaming with joy. He also heard their voices.

I am allowed to live again, he said to himself. *I am really going to offer my life to Jesus this time,* he vowed and felt deep gratitude to God, who had given him a new life.

He thought again, *Was it a mere dream? What did Jesus mean by "Search for my heart and feelings; my time is approaching"? Did He mean something concrete by these words?*

Chuichi thought and thought again, but he could not get a clear answer. He told Father Minamida, the priest who had taught him the Catechism and had baptized him, about his dream. Father Minamida didn't seem to understand what those words meant, but he encouraged Chuichi. "How happy you are to see Jesus in your dream! Trust that Jesus loves you, and always keep it in your heart and constantly pray and seek for its meaning."

Separated Brothers

Becoming a Priest

In the ceremony of ordination, the bishop asks the candidate for the priesthood:

"Do you willingly vow to maintain celibacy the rest of your life so that you can freely love God and other people?"

The candidate is ordained only after answering "Yes."

This is something that should never be forced and should be chosen of one's own will. The road to priesthood in the Catholic Church is not easy. This is not only because one has to study philosophy and theology for at least six years: it takes just as long to become a medical doctor. It is because of the vow of celibacy.

It takes much courage to become a priest in any religion. In order to become a Catholic priest, one has to vow celibacy for the rest of one's life, which is just as difficult in any other sect of Christianity or in other religion which obliges celibacy for the priesthood. Many young people enter Catholic Seminary wishing to become priests, but only a small number of people actually become priests.

Indeed, there are some who lack aptitude for leadership or for loving and serving others, but many people think that one of the major reasons why few people either wish to become priests or why many abandon the priesthood is because of the celibacy requirement.   The celibacy of priests holds the danger of bringing about various sexual problems such as homosexuality, sexual abuse of children, and hidden relationships with women. Some Catholic believers and priests are calling for the abolishment of celibacy for priests, saying that it is out of date and that Jesus Christ himself did not demand celibacy of his disciples. However, at present, if one wants to become a Catholic priest, one must accept celibacy.   In spite of the high hurdle of celibacy, it is a fact that there have always been some who have tried to become priests. What attracts people to the vocation of the priesthood? Do they lack anything as men? Or do they sense something of such great value that it is worth the sacrifice of staying celibate for one's entire life?

Of course, its value is only known to those who have become priests. But when we consider that there are some who abandon the priesthood, there may be many who do not find this value even after becoming priests. For many candidates for the priesthood, vowing lifelong celibacy does not merely mean keeping celibacy in the future, but may also involve sacrificing a beloved in the present. Some have broken engagements and entered the seminary. Whether we consider that a call from God and Christ or self-centered behavior may depend on interpretation. But the priests themselves, at least, think that they have chosen to love God instead of loving a person. Even if they convince themselves that it was a call from God, naturally they go through the pain and struggles of sacrificing their love, and if the ones they love have a hard time accepting it, the pain of having hurt the loved one remains.

Seiichi had such a thorn in his heart.

An Incomprehensible Confrontation

Seiichi entered a Protestant, not a Catholic university, and studied theology. As it was a Christian university, of course, there were many things in common with the Catholic Church, but there were also many differences. Seiichi began to learn Protestant theology perhaps as a counterpoint to having been raised in a devout Catholic family.

Chuichi had told Seiichi why he became a Catholic and how he had miraculously overcome his cancer by God's grace after hovering between life and death. This greatly helped Chuichi develop faith in God and Jesus. Soon, Seiichi naturally wanted to believe in the same Catholic faith that his father experienced, believed in, and had convictions about.

Seiichi met many good people in the Catholic Church. They were serious, kind, and had warm personalities. But as he grew up to be a junior high school student and later a high school student, he began to struggle with various questions about the Catholic faith and the Catholic Church. He did not think that the Catholic teachings were wrong; nor did he lose respect for his father. He simply had questions.

He was particularly puzzled as to why there were so many sects criticizing and battling each other within the Christian church. Why were there Catholics, Protestants, Anglicans, and Orthodox, even though they all believed in the same Jesus Christ? The issue of schism was a big question for Seiichi. By the time he began to prepare for the entrance examination to university, he wanted to study Christian theology from a perspective other than the Catholic one. "There is no problem with studying theology, but why does it have to be Protestant theology and not Catholic theology?" His parents and the priests and Sisters who were close to him questioned him. Some openly opposed him. A Sister said to him seriously, "I will pray to God that you do not pass the entrance examination."

As he heard these words he thought, *Is it such a bad thing for a Catholic to study Protestant theology?*

Seiichi found it difficult to understand why there were hundreds of different denominations within the same Christian church and why they were battling with each other. Staying just within the Catholic Church had seemed like being in a very small world to Seiichi. Although he was surprised at the unexpectedly strong opposition expressed by the people around him, the more he was opposed, the more he thought it necessary to study Protestant theology. He decided to study it regardless of opposition.

Since the Reformation in 1517, Catholics and Protestants had been denouncing each other as anti-Christs or heretics, and sometimes they had even killed one another. It took almost 450 years before the Catholic Church finally called the Protestant church "a separated brother." It had only been a few years since the Second Vatican Council, so perhaps the words of the Sister hoping he would fail his entrance exams were understandable.

When Seiichi attended the Protestant theology classes and services, he was at first perplexed to find that the prayers and the hymns were different from those of the Catholic Church, although both were Christian. He felt comfortable with the familiar Catholic prayers and holy songs, but he felt strange and uncomfortable with the Protestant prayers and hymns.

He knew that such feelings came from his Catholic background and not from God or Christ. He knew that in his mind, but he had to struggle very much in his heart before he could overcome those strange feelings and feel as comfortable as he did in the Catholic Church. However, most of the professors were pastors, and he found in them gentle personalities and deep love for their students. Seiichi benefited much from coming into direct contact with the Protestant professors as well benefitting from their lectures.

While Seiichi studied Protestant theology at university, he belonged to the Catholic Bible Study Circle as an off-campus activity. He felt he needed to study both.

He lived for the activities of the Catholic Society. His world expanded by playing a central role in this group. For activities, they volunteered every Saturday evening to raise funds for severely handicapped people; they held gatherings to read the Holy Bible and other Christian books; and they had discussions on faith in God or various problems in life. They also promoted mutual friendship through recreation.

The Catholic Society was an association of university students of the Catholic Church, and there were branches in different universities. In Kyoto in those days, not every university had its own branch, and Catholic students from several universities gathered together. They met in one of the rooms of the Kyoto Catholic Cathedral in Kawaramachi Oike. There were about thirty members, but it was a small group with less than ten "regulars".

Beyond a Dream that Never Comes True

An Encounter

April 1992; Kyoto, Japan

Seiichi Yamamoto liked the "Philosophy Road" at this time of the year, after the cherry☐ blossom season when there were fewer tourists.

Because new members from outside Kyoto joined the Catholic Bible Study Circle, they went sightseeing in Kyoto every year to welcome and get acquainted with the new freshmen members. The welcoming event that year consisted of gathering at Nanzenji, walking the "Philosophy Road", and visiting the Silver Pavilion.

However, the main event was having a pleasant talk at a tea room located on the Philosophy Road. It was named Philosophy Road because Kitaro Nishida, a philosopher, was said to have walked along this road as he meditated.

The road was always crowded with tourists during the cherry blossoms season and the time when the leaves turned red. The cherry blossoms on both sides of the canal where pure water runs are beautiful and breath-taking.

Seiichi thought that the season when the tree leaves were green and there were fewer people, after mid April, was more suited to the name Philosophy Road than when the road was full of people during the full-bloom cherry blossom season.

The cherry leaves had changed colors from yellowish-green to dark green, and spring sun rays shone over the fourteen members, including the new members, of the Bible Study Circle. They walked the Philosophy Road by twos and threes. The shiny sun rays glistened over them as though they were teasing them.

There was a woman member who was walking alone some distance behind the group. Seiichi noticed her and looked back. Sun rays shone over her under a tree, and she was looking up as if she was taking a deep breath. She was surrounded by the green leaves and then she slightly spread her arms. She had a childlike expression on her face. She seemed refreshed being under the green tree leaves and at the same time she seemed lonely and not quite capable of participating in conversation with other members of the circle. Seiichi knew her name was Kokoro Ueno.

Seiichi slowed down and waited for Kokoro to come closer to him.

"Is this your first time in Kyoto?" he asked.

"No. I grew up in Kyoto."

"Then this tour isn't anything new to you, is it?"

"Yes, it is. I've never been here before. It's truly a nice place."

"I live in Sagano. Where do you live?"

"Fushimi."

"Really?"

Seiichi thought that something about Kokoro's closed profile, looking down, communicated that she didn't want to be asked any further questions, and he changed the subject.

Kokoro had visited the room of the Catholic Society with her friend Yumiko Okada from the women's university she attended. She was standing behind her friend, who said, "We would like to join the Catholic Society." Kokoro didn't say a word. Kokoro's reserve   impressed Seiichi.

Seiichi had reserved an elegant tea room located halfway along the Philosophy Road for this day. It was a small place that became full when all the members entered. Seiichi, who was the leader, ushered everyone to their seats. Kokoro Ueno, who came in last, ended up sitting next to Seiichi.

When all the orders were taken, they resumed the conversation they had started while walking to the tea room. When more than ten members got together, it was difficult for all of them to discuss the same topic. It was much more so on this day because it was not a meeting or a study session. It was a welcoming party for the new members.

Kokoro, who didn't join the conversation, seemed to be quietly smiling at each member. Sometimes she looked at the scenery outside and seemed to be thinking about something.

Seiichi was talking with everyone and yet he felt he shouldn't desert her. He said, "I'm sorry if I asked you something you didn't want to be asked."

"Oh, I'm sorry I didn't answer you properly. To tell you the truth, I don't have parents. I was brought up in an orphanage from the time I was an infant."

"Is that so? Do you still live in an orphanage?"

"No. When I was in the ninth grade, I was taken to my present parents' place."

"Do you mean you were adopted?"

"Yes. They are not my real parents. Recently, my stepfather hasn't been well."

"I'm sorry to hear that. I'm not sure how I can help you, but please talk to me if you need any help."

"Thank you."

Just then one of the members cried out loudly, "There's a bush warbler!"

Everyone looked out the window and asked, "Where is it?" They started making such a commotion that Seiichi's conversation with Kokoro ended there.

After that, Seiichi met Kokoro a few times a month at their Bible Study Circle. They only exchanged greetings. They never spoke alone, and time passed.

An Extreme Emptiness

Although Seiichi was absorbed in the activities of the Catholic Society, he somehow found emptiness in his heart. There were various reasons for it, but first of all, it was perhaps because he had not found his purpose or direction in life at all.

It could have been, too, because he had not yet met a friend he could truly trust with his heart. Even if he shared his feelings in his circle, he felt lonely afterward. He could not touch anyone's heart, and no one felt as he did.

"Is it difficult to truly understand each other even when we have the same Catholic faith? Or am I simply yearning for something that can never come true?"

Seiichi asked himself the same question many times. Then, though, there was a time when he felt free from emptiness and experienced peace in his heart. It was at a crossing in Shijou Kawaramachi in downtown Kyoto. He fund-raised there every Saturday evening for the severely handicapped people, calling for donations with a megaphone in his hand. He didn't know why, but for some reason that was the only time he could feel the presence of God and attain peace in his heart. Thus, he continued fund-raising earnestly every Saturday.

Other members who had initially participated in the volunteer work with him became busy with their studies or lost enthusiasm. As the number of participants decreased, Seiichi couldn't help noticing that there was a big gap between his heart and the hearts of other members. For the others, the meetings of the Catholic Society or the fund-raising were not something they needed to be eagerly involved with. For them, examinations and finding employment in the immediate future were more important issues or they valued the time they spent with a lover.

In those days, the "bubble" economy had burst in Japan, but its effects were still felt. Since the late 1980s, people in Japan were restless and light-hearted because of the skyrocketing "bubble" economy. The excess money was spent on real estate and art, and prices skyrocketed. The coquettish laughter of women flew back and forth in amusement areas. Young people spent their days in discos and at parties. Seiichi's university was no exception. There were many couples on campus, walking arm in arm or cuddling together. There were many women students who dressed scantily in order to attract the attention of men. It was a frivolous time.

The number of members who came to the meetings decreased, and even fewer members participated in fund-raising.

Yet Seiichi never stopped the Circle activity, and he kept on fund-raising. By doing so, he was perhaps searching for the image of Jesus in himself that he was sure was there, although sometimes it was shaky.

"Am I different from others? Why is it that I only feel peace in my heart here? Why don't others feel the same way?"

Seiichi felt empty and lonely. Although he had already been given informal assurance of employment as a teacher at a mission school, he was in great anxiety when he thought of accepting that job offer as he had planned. The future seemed dim and inscrutable.

A Letter

Summer vacation ended, and a new semester began. One day, Seiichi came home from university and found a letter in the mail box. It was written on stationery with a Japanese bellflower design on it, and the envelope was handmade Japanese paper. It was from Kokoro Ueno. She sometimes showed up in the Circle activity and listened attentively to what the others talked about, but she seldom talked herself.

"What has happened? Does she have a problem?" Seiichi wondered as he opened the letter.

"+Peace of the Lord

Dear Seiichi Yamamoto,

Please forgive me for writing to you so abruptly. You must be very surprised. To tell you the truth, ever since we talked on the Philosophy Road, I have been very attracted to you, and my heart has been troubled every day. I honestly don't know where this feeling comes from. I'm not certain if this is a romantic feeling or something different. I wonder why I told you about myself, something that I had never told anyone before. It seems that I can be honest with you. Later, every time I saw your sad expression when I attended the Bible Study Circle, I wished I could be of some support to you and this thought became more intense each time I saw you. Then I realized that when I think like that, I feel peaceful."

As Seiichi read the letter, his heart beat stronger and faster. The letter continued:

"I respect you very much, but I don't think that is all. I somehow feel that I must see you personally. With every ounce of courage I have, I decided to write to you. If you can fulfill my wish, would you please see me personally rather than at the meeting room of the Catholic Bible Study Society?

I look forward to hearing from you.

Sincerely,

Kokoro Ueno

Seiichi had never gone out with anyone before. He had previously received several letters from women university students consulting him about the Bible Study Circle or he had listened to them talk about their problems. But this was the first time he had ever received such a personal letter. Seiichi was surprised. At the same time, he realized that it must have taken Kokoro, who was so reserved, a lot of courage to write such a letter. He could almost feel the struggle and the pain she had gone through.

He read the letter many times. Each time he read it, two incompatible thoughts battled in his heart. One of them made him feel happy about what the letter said and suggested to him that he should go out with her. The other was far more troubling.

Seiichi had been feeling more and more lonesome because his friends were getting more distant from him. Because of this, the letter consoled him. Although he had never been conscious of it, he now saw that something in Kokoro attracted him. After reading her letter, Kokoro Ueno became very vivid to him. He started to remember some of her mannerisms, words, and facial expressions, one after another. Now that he knew that she cared for him, it seemed to him that he understood the feeling underneath all of them. At that moment Kokoro became adorable and precious to him.

Someone loves me.

When he thought thus, he began to think that he should pursue this relationship. He felt that his problems and struggles were somehow fading away, dissolved by a sweet sensation he had never experienced before. He had the urge to stay in that delicious world and go further into it.

But his other thoughts told him, *You can't even solve your own problems, nor have you found your purpose of life. Can you fall in love now? Wasn't finding the purpose of life the most important thing for you? Didn't you bear solitude and emptiness all for that? Didn't you sacrifice friendships and various other things for it? If you choose to fall in love, wouldn't that deny the most important thing you believe in?*

The two thoughts violently battled in Seiichi's heart. The battle lasted all night, but in the end his second mind won. It was only a night, but it seemed like a long period of time for him.

He began to write back to Kokoro.

"+Peace of the Lord,

Thank you for your letter. You don't know how much your letter consoled my lonely heart. I truly thank you. I also thank you for having cared about me.

However, I am not the kind of a great person you think I am. I have problems in my heart. I cannot even like myself, and I have been struggling about it very much for a long time. I am not qualified to accept your love.

This may sound cruel, but you hardly know me, and you are only idealizing me. When you find out who I truly am, I am sure that you will not like me.

Above all, I still have not found the purpose of life, why I am living. I have lived until now believing that I should find it before doing anything else. I cannot give it up now. I don't know when I will find it, but I cannot stop making effort to search for it.

Please forgive me for not being able to fulfill your wishes. This doesn't mean that I don't like you. I may hurt you deeply, but please understand.

I pray that God's love will be with you always.

Sincerely,

Seiichi Yamamoto"

Although he was physically tired from staying up all night, Seiichi felt refreshed. He was no longer struggling in his heart, and he believed that he had made the right decision. Early autumn morning sun rays were beaming into his room.

Seiichi didn't expect any reply from Kokoro. He was wrong. He received another letter from her.

"+Peace of the Lord.

Dear Seiichi Yamamoto,

Thank you for writing back to me.

To be honest, I was shocked to read your letter. For a moment, I felt as though my whole body had frozen. But as you wrote in your letter, it is indeed true that I hardly know you.

However, I don't think that it is right of you to think that I like you because I don't know you well or that I am idealizing you and would dislike you if I knew who you really are. I think you struggle about your problems because your heart is much purer than others'. If you really had an ugly heart, you would not be aware of it. As I read your letter, I felt that the reason why I am attracted to you is because of your heart that tries to search for purity in such a way and because of your serious attitude about earnestly looking for the purpose of life.

So, please do not reproach yourself so much. Please give me a chance to get to know you. I believe that I would not dislike you if I knew you better.

Perhaps my expression, 'Please meet me personally,' may have caused some misunderstanding. I am only asking for an opportunity to know you as a human being. Please tell me more about God and Jesus as you know them.

In a sense, I have been walking a solitary path. I have problems I could not tell anyone before. Somehow, I feel that you would be able to understand me.

I will not do anything to prevent you from finding the purpose of your life. If you could grant my wish, please write me back.

Sincerely,

Kokoro"

A Separation

Seiichi was quite disturbed to receive the second letter from Kokoro, because he was so sure that Kokoro would give him up after reading his letter. Yet he could not find any reason this time to refuse to meet her. He was beginning to feel unbearably lonely, and this letter made him feel that she understood what he valued in life.

"She may be the only person who can understand my desire to search for the purpose of life."

Thus, he convinced himself to meet Kokoro.

It was on a Sunday afternoon. They decided to go see a movie together first and talk in a coffee shop afterward. They were going to see a love story. Kokoro chose the movie. After Mass in the morning, Seiichi attended a meeting of the youth association of the church and then took a bus that headed for Kawaramachi Sanjou in downtown Kyoto. As his body was shaken in the bus, his heart also wavered between wanting to see Kokoro soon and anxiety and fear about seeing her. Although he had denied falling in love, he had some yearning to be in love. To Seiichi, Kokoro was perhaps the only person able to understand him.

As he sat with Kokoro and watched the movie, he faced an unexpected and shocking reality. Although the beautiful scenes of the movie made him smile, his heart felt emptier than ever before.

The time alone with Kokoro was supposed to be sweet and pleasant, yet it turned out far differently. Where did this strange emptiness come from? This was not the kind of feeling a man should have on an occasion like this. This was not normal.

But in reality, this was how he felt, and the emptiness in Seiichi's heart grew stronger and stronger.

Seiichi struggled to understand. No one thought there was anything wrong in a man liking a woman, not even in Christianity. Seiichi couldn't think that it was wrong to look for some comfort in his relationship with Kokoro either. Indeed, he was beginning to cherish Kokoro in his heart. And yet, he still felt empty. He couldn't understand himself.

"I cannot talk with Kokoro feeling this way," he told himself.

Then suddenly, he remembered the announcement made after Mass at the church:

"Please come and help fund-raise for the prevention of AIDS in front of the Takashimaya Department Store in Shijou Kawaramachi this evening."

After the movie, he said to Kokoro without letting her say a word, "Ueno-san, I'm sorry. I'm very sorry. I suddenly remembered while seeing the movie that I was asked long ago to help fund-raising for the Prevention of AIDS this evening. I have to keep this promise by all means. I'm sorry, but could we talk some other time? I'm really sorry. It was a very beautiful movie. Thank you. Goodbye."

He finished talking and left Kokoro, who looked sad and seemed to want to say something more. He started to walk in the direction of Shijou Kawaramachi. When he looked back, Kokoro with pale face was still standing at the same place and was looking at him. Seiichi waved to her. Kokoro waved back. She was desperately trying to smile, but she was crying as she waved.

This was the last image he had of Kokoro, and it was imprinted in Seiichi's memory. This incident became a thorn stuck deep in his heart. His heart ached over it.

What a cold thing I'm doing, Seiichi had thought as he headed for Shijou Kawaramachi. Kokoro was already receding in his heart.

Then Seiichi was attacked by such an intense emptiness that he gave up all thought of caring for Kokoro. He could not figure out why he felt that way. It was so unbearable, he cried out as he started to run towards Shijou Kawaramachi.

"God!"

He realized that getting involved with Kokoro would make him feel emptier rather than resolve the emptiness in his heart. He also realized that he could not resolve the emptiness by himself.

God often consoled his lonely, empty heart when he was fund-raising for the physically handicapped or for the refugees at Shijou Kawaramachi.

If I go to Shijou Kawaramachi and help with the fund-raising, I may be liberated from this empty feeling, thought Seiichi and he ran desperately, squeezing his way through the crowd to reach the place.

But when he arrived at Shijou Kawaramachi in front of the Takashimaya Department Store, there was no one fund-raising, although it was way past the time to begin.

"Was it cancelled because no one came?" he murmured to himself. He helplessly sat on the guardrail at the edge of the street.

God, You are the only one I can depend on. I thought I could meet You here.

Seiichi was at a loss, thinking that now even God had abandoned him.

Everything seemed so vain.

He had no more strength to do anything.

He even thought that it was meaningless to live.

He couldn't hear the traffic or hear people talking as they passed him. His eyes were open, but he saw nothing.

A Call

Reunion with Father Minamida

How long had he sat on the guardrail in front of the Takashimaya Department Store? Seiichi came to himself suddenly when he heard a voice.

"Hello. Aren't you Seiichi Yamamoto?"

There was an old gentleman smiling as he stood in front of him.

"Father Minamida!"

It was the priest who had led his father Chuichi to encounter Jesus Christ and be baptized a Catholic.

"You remember me?"

"Yes."

Seiichi's father had told him many times about Father Minamida, and Sheiichi knew that he respected and trusted him very much. Seiichi himself had also met him when his family visited Father Minamida's church when he was a little child. He only vaguely remembered it, but his father had framed the picture of Father Minamida and Seiichi's family taken on that occasion, and it had been placed prominently in their home.

Seiichi had seen the picture many times, so he remembered the face of Father Minamida well. More than fifteen years had passed since then. Although Father Minamida had some gray hair, Seiichi thought that Father Minamida hadn't changed.

Seiichi remembered his father saying, "Father Minamida is responsible for an area facing the Sea of Japan, a few hours away from Kyoto by train. He has been working for the people of three small parishes for a few years now."

"How did you recognize me, Father?"

Seiichi was happy that Father remembered him.

"Well, I wasn't so sure, but I thought that it might be you, and I called your name. And it was you, and I was surprised, too. I am getting old and haven't been very well. I am often ill and haven't been able to come to Kyoto to attend the priests' conferences for a few years. But this time, I'm well enough to come and attend the conference. It's been three years since the last time I came to Kyoto. By the way, are you meeting someone here?"

"No. I came here because I heard that there was going to be fundraising here for the prevention of AIDS. There seems to be no one coming."

"Oh, is that so? I just found a book I was looking for and was thinking of having dinner somewhere so that I could take a break. If you have time, would you like to have dinner with me? I'd like to ask you about your parents."

The way Father Minamida talked made Seiichi sense that Father Minamida had really missed him and his family, and this made him want to have dinner with him. Of course, he had time, because he had planned to have dinner with Kokoro. He then felt pained about what he had done to Kokoro. He wondered what she had done after he left her. Did she get home safely?

Seiichi and Father went into a family restaurant. Seiichi didn't notice that Kokoro was there, hiding herself and watching them.

As they had dinner, Father began to talk about his health and the church he was working at in the country. Then Seiichi told Father about his family, since the priest inquired. Then somehow, he began to tell him about the emptiness in his heart. He also told him about Kokoro and why he was helplessly sitting on the guardrail in front of the Takashimaya Department Store in Shijou Kawaramachi and how he felt that God had abandoned him. Father Minamida kept nodding his head. He listened earnestly to Seiichi until Seiichi had finished talking.

Seiichi felt refreshed after telling Father Minamida everything that had weighed so heavily on his heart.

He asked suddenly, "Father, why did you want to become a priest?"

Father Minamida explained, "An American missionary, Father Emile Glucco, taught me the Catholic catechism, and I was baptized a Catholic. Six months after that, I collapsed, vomiting blood, and I was diagnosed with esophageal cancer. The doctor declared that I had only a few months left to live. He said it was too late to have surgery. All I could do was wait to die. I was in so much despair that I didn't have any energy left for anything."

Then one day when his mind was wandering in the depths of despair, Father Glucco who was concerned about him, came to consult him about something.

"Mr. Minamida, the Vatican Ambassador is coming to Kyoto in secret. What do you say? Would you guide him around Kyoto? He was actually a classmate of mine when I was studying in Rome. That's why he asked me to show him around Kyoto. Since I'm not very familiar with the geography of Kyoto, it's a little difficult for me. So I'm wondering if you could help me, since you were born and grew up in Kyoto. Of course, I will do the interpreting."

Minamida couldn't believe what he heard.

"What can be more honorable for me, having just been baptized, to be able to meet the Vatican Ambassador, a representative of the Roman Pope? Not only that, but I'm also asked to help him."

He was greatly moved in his heart, feeling that Father deeply loved and trusted him.

He must know others who are in better health and know Kyoto much better than me, he thought.

He understood on a profound level that Father Glucco was trying to console him and encourage him in the best way he could, because he was in despair after receiving a death sentence. He felt his eyes getting tearful. But it was clearer than anything else to Minamida that if he went around Kyoto, he would die sooner.

"I may die in the midst of it, but that doesn't matter. I would be quite satisfied if I could directly serve the representative of the Roman Pope, who is representing Jesus, at the end of my life. I would do it thinking that I am serving Jesus."

Minamida was thus determined and decided to accept taking the responsibility of guiding the Vatican ambassador around Kyoto. It was on the day of the Gion Festival, midsummer, and it was so hot and humid that they sweated even while keeping still. Minamida guided the Vatican Ambassador around the city of Kyoto for the whole day.

Two months passed after he performed that important mission. He could not forget the happy expression of the Vatican ambassador when he saw the beautiful Japanese culture, not only the Gion Festival but also the temples such as the Kinkakuji (Golden Pavilion), Ryouanji, and Kiyomizu Temple.

When Minamida thought of it, he felt as if Jesus, who knew his heart, was happy. He felt warm in his heart. He now thought that he could die happy, without regrets, and he began to prepare for his death. Meeting the Vatican ambassador gave him peace in his heart, and he accepted his imminent death. Minamida started to write his will to his family and friends. He also wrote Father Glucco a long letter, confessing the sins he had committed in his life, asking for God's forgiveness.

Shortly after that, something strange happened.

"I don't know what caused it, but I must take back my death proclamation," his doctor told Minamida. Minamida's condition was improving.

In medicine in those days, esophageal cancer could not be cured without surgery, chemotherapy or radiation treatment. The physician in charge ran many tests and examined Minamida again.

He said to him, looking somewhat embarrassed, "The Christ you say you believe in may have caused a miracle and saved you. That is the only thing I can tell you, but I am so happy for you. We still have to monitor you, but you might be able to go home again. Indeed, strange things do happen in this world. I should also ask Father Glucco to tell me about Mr. Christ."

As he joked, he looked deep into Minamida's eyes and held his hands tightly.

"Can such a strange thing be really true?"

Minamida shivered to think that something he had only read about in the biographies of saints was actually happening to him. He then remembered the words of Jesus in the Bible: "Those who seek to live would die and those who would die would live" (Matthew16: 25).

"What would have happened if I had declined the request from the Father Glucco and had not guided the Vatican ambassador? I couldn't help thinking that life is mysterious. I was still a bachelor then and decided to offer the rest of my life to God as a priest out of gratitude to Christ."

He has been a priest for nearly thirty years, and the number of persons that he led to the Catholic Church and baptized, including Chuichi, was no less than eight hundred.

"By the way, Seiichi, have you ever thought of becoming a priest?"

"No, I haven't. I've never thought about it."

It was true, Seiichi had never thought of becoming a priest until then.

"Each person has a precious value and cannot be replaced by anyone else. God has given a purpose of life to each and every person that can only be realized by that person. We feel empty when we haven't found our purpose of life, or when we are not living in the direction of realizing that purpose. Usually, there is a big gap between the God we know and the actual God. Seiichi, after I listened to you, I suddenly thought, 'God may perhaps be calling Seiichi to the road of priesthood.' Of course, I may just be thinking too much. But if you don't mind, would you think about it a little?"

These words pulled at Seiichi's heartstrings. He felt something very important regarding the purpose of life he had been searching for slowly rising from the bottom of his heart.

Diary

Seiichi went home that day and wrote in his diary for a long time.

"I may have met God today. Until today, I probably had an unconscious image of God as a glorious existence far distant from the struggles and sorrows of human beings, who is never influenced by human emotions.

However, God might be with us when we suffer and struggle. In fact, God was accompanying Father Minamida closely and was suffering and struggling with him.

Today, I feel that this God needs me and is calling me. God is calling me. Why did I never realize it before? This was where my life was supposed to be headed, and I was looking in other places. I was not searching for God where He was; I was searching for Him where He wasn't. Thus, I was feeling empty, and I even felt that God had abandoned me. I thought that God couldn't be with me or love me as I was. However, God was with me and loved me as I was."

When he finished writing, he remembered the time he ran towards Shijou Kawaramachi, crying out in his heart: "God!"

He continued to write:

"I needed to have love for God that depends only on God and earnestly yearns only for God and nothing else. God revealed Himself to me when I had nothing else other than Him to depend on. This encounter with God is what I have been searching for. This was the precious thing I needed above anything else."

When he finished writing in his diary, he was surprised to think how the world in his heart could change in just one day. The emptiness in his heart had disappeared. Warm and pleasant tears touched his cheeks.

* * *

It was pitch-dark outside the airplane window. Seiichi's eyes, reflected on the window, were shining. As he watched his face reflected on the window, he saw lights here and there below the plane. To Father Yamamoto, those lights seemed like lights of hope, enveloping and melting away the sins of people. He thought that he could start again with a fresh mind to let people know about the happiness of going back to God's will. Slowly, he fell asleep.

CHAPTER 3
Misunderstanding

Reunion

Kokoro and Sister Theresa

August 2007; Kyoto

Father Yamamoto was going up the hill to the convent of the Missionaries of the Consolation of the Sacred Heart of Jesus. He was sweating. The mountains were glowing with the setting summer sun.

Sister Theresa was the Sister who had a key for solving the issue of the Cross Immolation Syndrome. Somehow Father Yamamoto felt depressed at the thought of seeing her, but the beautiful mountains in Kyoto and the fresh air of Kitayama made him forget it for a moment. Japan had a kind of beauty different from Europe.

Father Yamamoto had heard many times in the past about Sisters and believers who claimed to have received revelations from Jesus or Mary. In most cases, Jesus had not really appeared. Some had schizophrenic hallucinations; some were acting out in order to get attention, or they were led astray by their own overheated imaginations. That was why Father Yamamoto couldn't help being skeptical when it came to such things.

He didn't believe this time either that the Sister had really received a revelation from Jesus. At the same time, his conscience was pricking him for having such doubts before even meeting her and listening to her. So as he walked up the slope, he prayed in his heart that he could successfully accomplish this investigation. Summer in Kyoto was hot, even in the evening, and climbing all the way up the slope was not easy.

When he rang the bell of the convent, Sister Hostia welcomed him inside. A lamp was lit in the small and simple reception room where he was shown. A woman, possibly Sister Theresa, was already there, waiting.

"Father Yamamoto is here," said Sister Hostia, and she opened the door of the reception room. When Father Yamamoto went into the reception room, Sister Theresa, who was bowing, raised her head.

Father Yamamoto was at a loss for words.

"Amazing! What a quirk of fate!"

Sister Theresa was Kokoro Ueno.

Who could have imagined it? Father Yamamoto suppressed his surprise.

Sister Hostia introduced Sister Theresa to Father Yamamoto and served them tea and chatted with them for a while. Then she left the room, leaving them alone.

They had not met since Seiichi had left her on the street after watching a movie with her, and Father Yamamoto knew nothing about Kokoro's life after that. He had thought that she would be married to someone by now and raising a happy family.

"What a cold thing I did to her!"

He cried this out in his heart, seized with regret for having done such a cruel thing. Kokoro had been on his mind ever since. Although he never did anything about it, he had suffered many times, thinking of finding her and apologizing. No one knew how much he had suffered.

There was an oppressive silence. Soon, Father Yamamoto plucked up his courage and began to speak.

"I did a terrible thing to you back then, leaving you alone in front of the movie theater. I don't know how I can apologize to you. I don't think I can be forgiven, but I have always wanted to apologize to you. I'm sorry," said Father Yamamoto, and he bowed and kept still, as if he were a defendant waiting for the verdict.

In Silence

"Father Yamamoto, please raise your head," said Sister Theresa in an unexpectedly gentle tone of voice.

"Don't you have resentment against me?"

"No, I don't have any resentment against you. Rather, I need you to forgive me."

Father Yamamoto looked dubious, unable to understand.

Sister Theresa continued, "I wrote in my letter that I was not expecting to have any romantic relationship with you. I had thought that I had a very pure feeling. So, indeed, I was very hurt at that time, and I did have a grudge against you. Later, as I studied the Holy Bible and the teachings of Jesus more in depth and looked into my own heart more closely, I began to recognize the selfishness, ugliness, and sinfulness in my heart.

"In the end, I came to understand that you were not wrong and that I was wrong. Although I had not wished to see you solely because of romantic feelings, I realized later that there was a selfish expectation in the bottom of my heart. So, please don't blame yourself anymore."

Father Yamamoto was grateful for her words. He had suffered about the incident for a very long time. Although this was something totally unexpected, he had to thank God for giving him the opportunity to apologize and also to find out that she did not hold any resentment against him. Had he not been given such an opportunity, he would have had to suffer about it for the rest of his life and would never have been liberated from a sense of guilt.

"I still believe that you didn't write that letter just because of an emotional reason."

With these words of Father Yamamoto, Sister Theresa smiled.

"Thank you very much. However, there is one more thing I must confess to you and ask for your forgiveness for."

"You need to confess to me?"

"Yes."

Father Yamamoto could not figure out what Sister Theresa was trying to say.

"A while after you left me, saying that you had to go to Shijou Kawaramachi for fund-raising for the prevention of AIDS, without letting me say a word, I also went to Shijou Kawaramachi."

"Of course, you weren't aware of it. I didn't like myself for doing it, but I had to go and see whether what you had said was true or not. I had to know if you really left me to do the fund-raising."

"Was that so? But I am not qualified to be asked for forgiveness."

"Just by talking about it to you, I feel something has been dispelled, and I feel better. Also, what you said was true."

"But how did you find out that it was true? I wasn't fund-raising then."

"Indeed, you were not fund-raising, and there was no one fund-raising there. But I knew intuitively that you hadn't lied to me. I saw you sitting on the guardrail in front of the Takashimaya Department Store, looking so disappointed."

The memory of that scene revived in Father Yamamoto's mind.

"I couldn't understand at all why you looked so despondent after seeing the movie with me. I was very shocked. I wasn't able to comfort your loneliness or emptiness but rather I made them worse, and this humiliated me. I was disgusted with myself and felt hopeless."

"Now, I really understand how you must have felt. I'm truly sorry for what I did to you," Father Yamamoto said in an apologetic manner.

"But after that, I saw your face brighten up as an elderly priest spoke to you, and you responded to him. When I witnessed it, I realized that you had been suffering on a level totally different from mine, a world which I couldn't enter. It's difficult to express it in words. I understood then that what you were seeking and trying to love was not someone else or any woman, but it was Jesus and God.

After that, you both went into a family restaurant, didn't you? And a few weeks after that, I found an article in the Catholic newspaper that said you had entered the seminary to become a priest. When I read it, I felt lonely, thinking that you would be gone somewhere I could not reach. At the same time, I remember, I was somehow convinced that it was right for you, and I was able to accept it."

As she spoke, Sister Theresa convinced Father Yamamoto that she truly did not have any resentment against him. He was also surprised at how well she understood his state of mind at that time. Just as she described, his life had completely changed by meeting Father Minamida, and it was true that he realized on that day that what he had been really searching for was not love for a person but rather love for God.

Yet it still was true that Father Yamamoto had deeply hurt Kokoro, and he thought that he would never forget how he had made her suffer. He also felt that Kokoro may have expressed herself in such a way out of kindness to him, to relieve him of his struggles.

Nevertheless, he was grateful for her good intentions and he also realized they had to move on to the main issue. Sister Hostia would never even dream that the two were talking about such a personal matter. They were not doing anything wrong, but now, considering their status as a priest and a nun, they certainly could not be too careful.

"Sister Theresa, I thank you for your thoughtfulness. You don't know how much you have relieved me. Thank you so much," said Father Yamamoto, and he deeply bowed to Sister Theresa again.

"The same goes for me," said Sister Theresa, and she also bowed her head.

There was a silence for a while between them, but it was not at all oppressive. They both needed some time to tell themselves to stop talking about the past. Of course, they did want to talk more about their youthful days and their lives since then. However, in silence, they were trying to confirm with each other in their hearts that they must deny such a desire. This caused some lonesomeness and pain in their hearts. Yet, in spite of that, they felt something warm and tender surrounding them.

Beyond a Distant Time

"Do You Remember Me?"

"May I now go on to the main subject?" Father Yamamoto broke the silence with a somewhat tense voice.

"Yes, of course," said Sister Theresa, repositioning herself in her chair.

"Are you aware that I came here today to interview you about the revelation you received from Jesus?"

"Yes, I am."

"Would you tell me about it? Also, I need to record our conversation in order to make a report on it. May I?"

"Yes, you may."

Father Yamamoto remembered the occasions when he interviewed Sisters with similar problems in the past. In most cases, he was irritated and sometimes felt unpleasant as he listened to them. He often found it difficult to suppress such feelings while listening to them all the way to the end.

This time, the person he was interviewing was someone he had liked in the past, and he did not find any schizophrenic or abnormal behavior in her. Yet, she was still a patient of the Cross Immolation Syndrome, who might be an important key for resolving it.

Father Yamamoto turned on his voice recorder, seated himself again, and began to ask questions.

"I'm probably not so spiritually keen, and I have never dreamed of Jesus, nor have I heard his voice. Did you hear Jesus' voice?"

"Yes."

"Did he speak in Japanese?"

Father Yamamoto thought that he was asking a silly question, and he suppressed a wry smile.

"Yes, I heard it in Japanese. But it was different from an ordinary voice."

"How was it different?"

"It sounded like something I heard within myself, and yet at the same time, it didn't seem so."

"I see. And what did Jesus tell you?"

"He asked me, 'Do you remember me?'"

These words were interesting enough to Father Yamamoto, but he tried not to express it on his face and went on asking questions.

"Has Jesus appeared to you before?"

"Yes, though you may not believe it."

Sister Theresa began to tell him about her background and her strange encounter with Jesus. Father Yamamoto quietly listened to her.

A Baby in a Basket

Sister Theresa was an orphan. Just after birth, a Sister found her abandoned in a basket placed in front of The Home of the Sacred Heart, a children's home run by the Catholic Missionaries of the Consolation of the Sacred Heart of Jesus. She was only a few weeks old. The situation was reported to the police, and they looked for her mother, but she was never found. So the Sisters decided to keep her with them in The Home of the Sacred Heart and raise her. They named her Kokoro Ueno.

Sisters who vow to God to remain single for a lifetime cannot have their own children. However, they were happy to have Kokoro, feeling as if God gave her to them. It was perhaps because they could feel something in common with the Virgin Mary, who is believed to have conceived Jesus without any sexual relationship with a man. Perhaps it was simply motherly instinct, which remained unconsciously within them even though they had vowed to stay single for life.

Of course, they could not express such emotions openly. That is to say, they tried not to express them. So, Kokoro was brought up in their children's home in the same manner as the other orphans. Kokoro was different from the others on only one point. Although they each had some unhappy reason for being there, some orphans had a few relatives who could help them. Kokoro had no one.

When it was time for the New Year's celebration or the Bon Festival, other children left the home to spend a few days with relatives. These were the loneliest and the bitterest times for Kokoro. At no other time did she realize as painfully that she was all alone in the world. She would then go to the church and spend her time there. She somehow felt at ease there, and strangely, she did not feel so lonely.

A Familiar Voice

"Kokoro, Kokoro."

Now an adult, Sister Theresa thought that someone was calling her by the name she had not been called since she became a nun when she heard this voice. Sister Theresa got up from her bed and turned on the light. She looked around her convent room, but there was no one there. It was a room, but all it had in it were a bed, a desk, an old narrow closet, a cross on the wall, an alarm clock, a light, and a small bookshelf. It was a very small room—only a four-and-a half tatami size.

"Someone may be calling me at the door."

She got out of her bed and quietly opened the door, but there was no one in sight as she looked down the long corridor.

"What time can it be?"

She looked at the clock at her bedside. It was only a little after four in the morning. From the window, with the curtain narrowly drawn open, she could dimly see the scenery outside. It was May, but it was still dark before dawn. She listened closely, all ears, but all she could hear was the wind rustling the leaves.

"Was it my imagination or was it a dream? I really thought I heard a voice."

Sister Theresa stayed in doubt for a while but she decided to go back to sleep again. There was still some time before the convent's morning prayer meeting that started at five thirty in the morning.

She slept for some time after that, but she was again awakened by a voice calling her name. She checked the corridor again but found no one.

"This is strange."

Sister Theresa was wide-awake, and she knelt down in front of the cross on the wall. She wasn't exactly praying but she stared at the face of Jesus on the cross for a while. Then, again, she heard a voice calling her.

"Kokoro, Kokoro."

It was that indistinct voice. She wasn't sleeping this time, so she was sure that it wasn't her imagination. It had a strange tone. It was tender and warm, yet it was different from ordinary words.

She could not tell where the voice came from. She thought it came from somewhere in her heart. This strange experience made her a little uneasy, but somehow she was not frightened. The voice sounded familiar to her, as though she had heard it somewhere before.

"I might have heard it somewhere," she thought. She tried to recollect memories of her past to discern whose voice it was.

"Kokoro is here. Who are you?" she responded.

The minute she asked the question, she suddenly remembered clearly a memory from her childhood that she had forgotten for a long period of time.

A Secret Shared with the Infant Jesus

It was when Kokoro was five years old. She was too young to know what it was to pray, but she would feel consoled when she went to the chapel and watched the image of Jesus on the cross or gazed at the statue of the Virgin Mary and her Child at the left side of the altar.

The Infant Jesus, who was carried by the Virgin Mary with an affectionate expression on her face, held a ball with a cross in his hand. The ball was actually the earth, and the cross was in the center of the earth. The Infant Jesus was holding it like a toy. It expressed that Jesus accomplished the salvation of humankind by his death on the cross and that he became the true king and ruler of the world. Kokoro liked that statue of the Virgin Mary and Child. The Virgin Mary carrying the Infant Jesus seemed to have some grief in her facial expression, but she also looked very tender.

As she looked at it, Kokoro suddenly thought, *Did my mother who gave birth to me have such a tender look on her face?*

There was a very unusual version of the painting *The Annunciation* on the wall at the right side of the chapel. The well-known painting depicts the scene when the Archangel Gabriel announces to the Blessed Virgin Mary that she will conceive the Messiah. But in this sacred painting, in addition to the usual motif, the Infant Jesus sent by God, the Father, was depicted on the right side of the painting, flying towards the Blessed Mary with a cross on his back.

The painting was trying to express that the Savior Lord Jesus was born with God's predestined plan to be crucified for the redemption and the salvation of humankind.

One day Kokoro was kneeling and praying in front of the statue of the Blessed Virgin Mary and the Child.

"Kokoro, Kokoro."

She heard an Infant calling her name. She was surprised, and she opened her eyes and looked around, thinking there might be some other child there. And then, when she looked back at the statue of the Blessed Virgin Mary and the Child, she doubted her eyes. The Infant Jesus was missing from the arms of the Blessed Virgin Mary. She looked around for him, and there he was, standing on the left side in front of the altar. He was smiling. Soon he began to walk towards Kokoro, holding that ball with a cross. He came over to her.

"Kokoro, let's play together."

She was much astonished and perplexed, but she was very happy.

"How are we going to play?" she asked him back with an excited heart.

"Let's roll this ball."

"It won't roll well, because it has a cross on it. Don't you think it's impossible to roll it?"

"No. We can pull the cross out, because it's not necessary."

Kokoro hesitated a little. Since she had been taught by priests and Sisters many times that the cross was very precious, even her very young heart resisted pulling it out. Seeing her hesitating, Jesus looked a little sad.

"I really want to take it off, even just for a little while as I play with you."

Kokoro felt pained, seeing Jesus pleading with her with serious eyes, and she decided to cooperate with him.

"But it looks difficult to pull out."

"It may be difficult alone, but if we do it together, it'll be possible. We can get it done. Will you help me?"

"O.K."

Kokoro approached the Infant Jesus. Jesus held the ball, and Kokoro pulled on the cross, which was painted red. She pulled it many times, but the cross wouldn't come off.

"It's impossible. Let's give up and do something else."

"No. I really want to pull this off. It won't come off unless you really believe that it will come off. Do you really believe it?"

She felt a little ashamed, sensing that Jesus knew that she had not really believed it.

"O.K. I really believe it."

Jesus smiled.

"Then let's do it again."

This time, they placed the ball between the short iron bars which separated the altar from the seats. Jesus held the right part of the cross and Kokoro held the left part of it, and they pulled. Then, Kokoro really wanted to believe Jesus. She pulled with all her strength. And then, surprisingly, the cross came off the ball, and both of them fell on the floor. Their laughter echoed in the church.

"I have never felt so refreshed in my life," she said to herself. Then they played together, rolling the wooden ball on the red rug in front of the altar. The light coming in through the stained glass moved and showed various colors inside the church.

How much time passed? When she noticed, she was lying alone sleeping on the red rug in front of the altar. She immediately looked for Jesus and the ball without the cross, but she couldn't find either of them. The only thing she could find was the same statue of the Blessed Virgin Mary carrying the Infant Jesus holding a globe with a cross. She looked the same as before, and she was smiling at Kokoro.

A few weeks after that, another strange incident occurred. Kokoro was kneeling with her eyes closed at a seat right in front of the altar. After a while, she somehow thought that it was getting bright around her, and she opened her eyes.

There, right in front of her, stood the Baby Jesus, carrying a cross on his back! It was the Jesus painted in the painting of *The Annunciation*, which was hung on the right side of the church. Jesus spoke to Kokoro, who stared at him, her eyes opened wide.

"Kokoro, take this cross off my back, because it's heavy."

"O.K. I'll take it off for you."

She helped the Infant Jesus take the cross off his back without hesitation. It didn't come off easily, but as she repeatedly pulled it many times, she soon was able to take it off.

"Jesus had to carry the cross since he was small."

As she said so, she felt pity for Jesus, thinking that it must have been hard to carry a cross on his back ever since he was a small child.

"Thank you, Kokoro! I feel very light!"

The Infant Jesus seemed happy to have his cross taken off his back and to be free. He thanked Kokoro. Kokoro, who held the cross she had taken off Jesus' back in her hand, thought it was heavier than she had ever imagined, and she simply could not rejoice. Jesus asked Kokoro to put down the cross on the floor and play with him, and they played hide-and-seek and other games together.

"This was a lot of fun!" she told him when they were finished playing.

Jesus was smiling.

"I enjoyed it, too. But, Kokoro, this is a secret just between you and me."

"All right. But can we play together again?"

"We may able to see each other again some day."

"When will that be?"

Jesus did not answer. He just smiled.

Again, when she noticed, she was lying alone, sleeping on the red rug in front of the altar. She looked for Jesus as soon as she woke up, but the Infant Jesus was back in the original painting with the cross and no longer spoke to her. For quite a long period of time, she went to the chapel every day, hoping Jesus would appear and play with her again. However, Jesus never appeared to her again.

Kokoro did not understand what these strange incidents meant.

"Were they dreams?"

No, they weren't dreams. It was true she played with Jesus.

"But who would believe such a thing?"

She decided not to tell anyone that Jesus had played with her.

Since then, strangely, she stopped feeling lonely.

As time passed, her memory of spending time with the Infant Jesus sank deep in her heart and disappeared from her consciousness.

"I Want You to Understand My Heart"

"Kokoro, Kokoro!"

This familiar voice indeed had the same tone as the voice of the Infant Jesus who had called her that day in her childhood.

The minute she realized it, she cried in her heart, "My Jesus!"

After the day she played with Jesus, there was a difficult period of time when she was treated bitterly by others for being an abandoned child and also for being a Christian. She would pray earnestly to God and Jesus on such days, but it was difficult to feel that her prayers were heard. She tried to believe that Jesus was with her, but the fact that she had been an abandoned child was too big an obstacle for her to believe in the salvation given by God and Jesus. Being an abandoned child seemed like evidence to her that no one wanted her to be born, and her heart was weighed down by it.

Kokoro attended Mass, and she kept offering her prayers in the mornings and in the evenings, but she thought, *Jesus cannot be with me, because I am an abandoned child born from a sinful situation.*

When she reflected back, she thought that she always had such feelings deep in her heart, although she might not have been conscious of them. She thought that she had gradually become distant from Jesus as she grew up.

Nevertheless, Jesus appeared to her again, even after so much time and distance.

I had forgotten about the secret encounter with Jesus, but he came to see me, although I am so faithless and sinful.

She remembered the words of the Infant Jesus: "We may be able to see each other again someday."

That "someday" meant today!

The moment she thought thus, she felt something very warm all over her body, and tears started to fall. She let them fall and wet her cheeks for a while.

After a while, she heard Jesus' voice again.

"My heart has been misunderstood. I want my heart to be understood."

Jesus only said that much and disappeared, as if he didn't understand that Theresa wanted to talk more. There was silence, as if nothing had happened.

The First Thing Sister Theresa Understood

"Thank you for the interesting story," said Father Yamamoto when Sister Theresa finished speaking.

"Can such a thing really happen?"

In his heart, Father Yamamoto wasn't sure if he could really believe it, although he did not verbalize those misgivings.

"May I ask you some questions about what you have just told me?"

"Yes, please."

"Does 'I want my heart be understood' mean that he wants you to understand?"

"I felt that I was being asked to understand, but at the same time I felt that He wanted all those who believe in Him to understand."

"Did He say how His heart had been misunderstood?"

"No. He didn't mention anything about that."

"Do you know what that may mean?"

"I don't know what it means, but there was something I felt when I prayed about it. I'm not sure if it's correct."

"That's all right. Please tell me."

"I think He wants to tell us that people have misunderstood that Jesus should have become the king to make Jerusalem independent from the Roman Empire, even though he was sent to this world to be crucified and resurrect."

"Well, that has been said before, and it is not anything Jesus needs to ask for again."

"Yes, he does. Isn't it because that has been neglected in modern times? I can't express it well, but the secular trend of pursuing material richness, pleasure, and convenience is also found in the Church. I think that such tendencies share something in common with how the disciples couldn't understand the meaning of Jesus' death on the cross and how Peter was scolded 'Go away, Satan. You are thinking about man and not of God,' when he tried to prevent Jesus from going the way of the cross. (Matthew: 16:23).

"Modern times are difficult for every religion, not just for Christianity. The number of members leaving the churches has been increasing in the traditional Christian churches, including the Catholic Church, and it is a serious problem. There are more instances in which the church is influenced by the society than where society is influenced by the church."

"I see. Yes."

"That is why, I think, Jesus wants us to look again for the eternal salvation and joy brought about by his death on the cross instead of such external pleasures and happiness that are not eternal. That is why he has said that he wanted us to understand his heart."

Father Yamamoto couldn't make a judgment as to whether Sister Theresa's interpretation was correct or not. He had, however, a favorable impression about the calm and modest way she expressed it. Yet he couldn't see any relevance between what she said and the reports of other patients of the Cross Immolation Syndrome, who experienced nausea upon seeing the cross. He decided to ask her some more questions."

Against Her Own Will

"I'm going to ask you about when you feel nausea or actually vomit in front of the cross. How long has it been going on?"

"It started to happen about a year and a half ago."

"Did such phenomena occur before then at all?'

"Not at all."

"When does it happen?"

"It happens when I see a cross."

"Does it always happen when you see a cross?"

"No, not always, but I think it's beginning to happen more frequently."

"Normally, when someone feels nausea without any physical cause, such as food poisoning or a physical disease, there are some psychological reasons. For example, one feels sick and vomits from seeing blood. In your case, do you feel sick when you see a cross?"

"Yes, but I don't understand myself at all or why it suddenly started to happen. The cross was something very precious and adorable to me. I'm sure that it is the same for you, Father Yamamoto. Whenever I kissed the cross, or prayed holding a cross tightly in my hands, I always used to feel noble and sometimes had sweet and adoring feelings toward it.

"I never thought of feeling nauseous seeing a cross. That's why I feel very anxious and fearful about feeling nausea now, against my own will.

"Honestly speaking, it is a great joy, and I feel saved to have Jesus appear to me again, but because I feel nausea seeing a cross, I sometimes doubt if the Jesus who appeared to me was real or not."

Father Yamamoto thought that he could understand her anxieties and struggles.

"I didn't like myself having such doubts, and I struggled about it. I would feel better if I knew what was causing the nausea, but I have no idea. But when I remembered the voice of Jesus, the sweet memories revived, and I determined to continue to believe that the Jesus who appeared to me was the real Jesus. Then, strangely, I was able to look at my situation from a different angle."

"What do you mean by 'from a different angle'?"

"If I knew the meaning of it, then it would no longer be a true struggle. So, an incomprehensible struggle like this indeed may be, in a sense, a true struggle. I am going to accept this struggle as it is and appreciate it. I can now think this way."

The symptom of feeling nausea upon seeing a cross, a manifestation of the Cross Immolation Syndrome, initially gave Father Yamamoto an image of a sensational occult phenomenon. However, as he listened to Sister Theresa in person, that image began to fade. Father Yamamoto still couldn't understand why Sister Theresa felt nausea at seeing a cross, but he thought that it was not necessary to worry that Sister Theresa might have anything abnormal about her.

He remembered the words of Professor Jurgen Barthezar: "The original image of the cross was not sweet or adorable but rather disgusting and detestable."

He felt that if he told her about it, her anxieties and struggles might ease a little. But he thought that telling her about it was going beyond his responsibility at this point. He decided to refrain from telling her that.

Thus, his reunion with Kokoro Ueno, who was now Sister Theresa, who had an important key to solving the Cross Immolation Syndrome, ended.

Report at the Vatican

Report on the Sister's Background and the Revelation

November 2007; the Vatican

It was in mid-November when the third meeting for counteracting the Cross Immolation Syndrome was called. Father Yamamoto was nervous at having to give a presentation in English in front of many people.

"Now we will have Father Yamamoto make a report on Sister Theresa, Kokoro Ueno, whom we consider to have a key to resolving the Cross Immolation Syndrome. He is going to tell us about her symptoms and her background, her personality, the relationship she had with Jesus until now, and the revelation she received. Father Yamamoto, please begin."

Ushered in by Cardinal Stewart, Father Yamamoto first briefly reported on Sister Theresa's background. He described how she was abandoned soon after she was born in front of the Home of the Sacred Heart, a children's home run by the Congregation of the Consolation of the Sacred Heart of Jesus. He explained how she was taken in by the Congregation and brought up at the Home of the Sacred Heart with other orphans until she became a junior high school student. He spoke of how later, she was adopted by an older brother of Sister Hostia Ueno, the Director of the Congregation, but she came back to the Congregation after she finished college in order to become a Sister.

He then explained how she had been suffering from her symptom of feeling nausea at seeing a cross, which seemed to be part of the Cross Immolation Syndrome. Lastly, he reported as precisely as he could on how she met the Infant Jesus in her childhood and on the revelation she received recently from the same Jesus who had appeared to her long ago.

However, he refrained from revealing his personal relationship with her. It was not that he felt any guilt about it. He thought that if this revelation was really from Jesus himself, he was responsible for doing his best to make it as acceptable as possible to people in general. Therefore, he thought he should avoid creating any kind of misunderstanding that might negatively affect his influence or cause people to make unnecessary assumptions.

Following the report made by Father Yamamoto, the participants at the meeting asked questions. He answered them one by one.

"What was your personal impression of Sister Theresa? For example, did you find anything abnormal in her? Was she restless? Did she seem self-aggrandizing?"

"The impression I had of Sister Theresa is that she is quite normal. I didn't find anything abnormal in her attitude. She didn't seem to be an emotionally unstable person or someone who cannot control her own emotions. I thought that she understood the meaning of my questions well, and she answered them honestly. There was nothing self-aggrandizing or arrogant in her attitude. Rather, I had the impression that she was very reserved and modest."

"You mentioned that she was an abandoned child. Has it left any psychological trauma in her, or has it caused in her a habit of daydreaming or an inability to relate with others?"

"I consulted the Director of the Congregation, Sister Hostia, about that, and she said that there have been no such problems so far. She remarked that Sister Theresa would often pray alone in the church during her childhood, and that she prays more often than other Sisters, but that was not because she was avoiding others. It has been accepted favorably."

"Was there any medical reason for her symptom of feeling nauseous at seeing a cross?"

"She has consulted a number of physicians, but just as with the others with similar symptoms, no physiological cause has been found."

"What about a psychological cause?"

"She has consulted several clinical psychologists and psychoanalysts about it, but they have not found any psychological factor or trauma in her psychology or in her sub- consciousness."

"Do you believe what she said about how she played with the Infant Jesus and the revelation from Jesus as something that really happened?"

"I personally find it difficult to believe such a thing really happened. Initially, honestly, I couldn't believe it. However, I didn't get the impression at all that she was making up a story. As I listened to her more, I started to feel more strongly that, although it was beyond my experience and understanding, it may perhaps really have happened."

The question and answer session ended.

"Thank you, Father Yamamoto," Cardinal Stewart said. "Now, we would like to continue our discussion based on Father Yamamoto's report. If you have an opinion, please share it."

Some raised their hands.

"What you said about how Sister Theresa played with the Infant Jesus sounds to me like a story she fabricated."

A few others made similar comments, but then someone disagreed.

"I had a similar experience when I was about four years old," said the Italian Cardinal Pietro Marras. "I have never told this to anyone before, but hearing the discussion, I decided to share it with you in case it may be of some help. Of course, it is not exactly the same as her experience, but the Infant Jesus carried by the Blessed Virgin Mary appeared to me also when I was praying in the church alone and he played with me. It didn't happen just once; it occurred several times. So, I think what she said she experienced was not a story she made up and that it can indeed be true."

People were sighing and some were murmuring in the room. It was because these words were from Cardinal Marras, who was respected for his personality as well as his academic work. He was a professor of the Vatican Bible Research Institute was well-respected in the field of biblical criticism. No one had expected him to recount such an experience. It was interesting that no one dared to discuss the issue after that. Cardinal Marras had such moral authority that his comment was enough to convince the participants at the meeting that such a mysterious thing was indeed possible.

They had a lunch break and then resumed their meeting to discuss the content of Jesus' revelation to Sister Theresa.

A Modern Version of the Revelation of the Sacred Heart?

First, Father Yamamoto reported on how Sister Theresa interpreted Jesus' revelation: "My heart has been misunderstood. I want my heart to be understood."

"I will report on how Sister Theresa herself interpreted the revelation from Jesus. She interpreted Jesus' words from an extremely traditional Christian viewpoint. According to her explanation, the Jewish disciples at the time of Jesus believed that the one who would build the Kingdom of God on earth in a visible form was indeed the Messiah they awaited. Thus, they expected Jesus to actually rebuild the Kingdom of Jerusalem as a king. However, Jesus understood that his mission was to build an invisible eternal Kingdom of God brought forth by the redemption from sin and the salvation through the crucifixion and the resurrection. In this sense, the people at that time, including his disciples, did not understand Jesus' true heart and misunderstood his feelings.

"By the same token, in modern times, as Christianity became secularized, even Christians began to have strong tendencies to pursue material happiness such as riches, social status, and earthly pleasures. Thus, they no longer understand the value of true happiness and the invisible eternal salvation from sins brought by his death on the cross and the resurrection.

"Sister Theresa explained that such modern Christians misunderstand the heart of Jesus just as the people at the time of Jesus misunderstood the feelings of Jesus who had come to this world to die on the cross. The revelation, 'My heart has been misunderstood; I want my heart to be understood,' is a warning against the secularized modern Christians who lack gratitude for Jesus' supreme act of love, for his having suffered for the salvation of humankind and having offered his blood and flesh as redemption. Therefore, she interpreted that this revelation from Jesus was a modern version of the Revelation of the Sacred Heart to St. Margaret Mary Alacoque, which the Congregation which she belongs to looks to as the purpose of its foundation."

"Isn't that a correct interpretation?"

When someone remarked thus, more than two thirds of the people present applauded. They thought that Sister Theresa's interpretation of Jesus' cross was correct. Indeed, it reflected their own ideas about the cross.

"I hardly know anything about St. Margaret Mary Alacoque and the Revelation of the Sacred Heart," a Methodist pastor from Kenya interjected. "I'm sure that others who are not Catholic may not know about them either. If someone who knows about them well could explain to us, it would make it easier for us to follow the argument."

"May I?" Cardinal Michel André from France volunteered to explain. "St. Margaret Mary is French, and the devotion to the Sacred Heart of Jesus is strongly entwined in French consciousness. I think it would save us a lot of time if you could ask me questions you'd like to ask and I answer them. Would someone ask me a question?"

When Cardinal André said this, several hands were raised.

"Does 'the Sacred Heart' mean the heart of Jesus?"

"Yes, it does."

"Does it refer to the feelings of Jesus?"

"It's a little different from that."

"How is it different?"

"'The Sacred Heart' doesn't refer to the feelings or psychological state of a person in general as we think of it in modern times. Rather, it is deeply related to the feelings or the physical heart of Jesus who suffered and shed his blood on the cross out of his love for humankind."

"We often see paintings of Jesus' heart bleeding."

"Yes. All such paintings have Jesus' Sacred Heart as their motif. Most of the Western languages have used the same word for the heart as an organ and the invisible heart. This is because from ancient times, human emotion was thought to originate in the organ of the heart.

"The reason why Jesus' bleeding heart is revered is because it was thought that in the heart of Jesus, who died shedding blood on the cross for the redemption from sin and the salvation of humankind, resided his burning love for humankind.

"This is based on the verse in the Holy Bible, 'Blood and water were shed,' (John: 19:34) when Jesus was pierced in his side by a Roman soldier."

"That verse doesn't apply here, does it? Jesus was pierced on his right side and the heart is on the left side."

"Indeed, you are right, but Christianity since ancient times has interpreted that when Jesus' heart was pierced and his blood was shed, his side was cut open, and through this, a way for his feelings and his physical heart to be revealed to humankind was opened. That is why Jesus' heart and side have been used in the same sense. The side, the feelings, and the physical heart had the same meaning, so the blood shed from his side was interpreted as the blood shed from Jesus' heart. Therefore, Christianity has revered the bleeding Sacred Heart of Jesus as the symbol of the love of God and Jesus for humanity. A heart enveloped by a flame, a beaming heart, and a heart with a crown of thorns—all these have the Sacred Heart as the motif.

"St. Catherine of Sienna (1347-1380), who influenced the Pope in her day, had a vision of exchanging hearts with Jesus. She used the expression, 'the sweetness of having a shower of Jesus' blood'. The image of the blood shed from the side of Jesus on the cross, which may even seem grotesque to those who are not Christian, is a sweet and beautiful image from which they can feel the love of Jesus the Savior the most."

"When did the Revelation of the Sacred Heart begin?"

"'The Revelation of the Sacred Heart' refers to the revelation given by Jesus to a French nun, St. Margaret Mary Alacoque, in the 17th century."

"Please tell us more detail about this saint."

"She was born in 1647 in Lhautecour in old Burgundy of France. She joined the Visitation Convent at Paray-le-Monial, and she died in 1690 at the age of forty-three."

"What kind of revelation did Jesus give to her?"

"Jesus appeared to her in 1673, and he repeatedly appeared to her several times until 1675. Jesus was hurt and bleeding, and he revealed to her his loving heart toward humanity. He told her that humankind must compensate for their ingratitude for the love and the grace he had granted to them by expressing devotion to the Sacred Heart. He confided to St. Margaret Mary that her mission was to spread devotion to the Sacred Heart all over the world. This is what is called the Revelation of the Sacred Heart or the Appearance of the Sacred Heart."

"Did the Catholic Church accept it as a revelation from Jesus right away?"

"St. Margaret Mary was initially not believed, and she was persecuted, but a priest who was her spiritual director, St. Claude de la Colombière of the Jesuits (1641- 1682), advocated that the revelation she had indeed did come from Jesus himself. Then the devotion to the Sacred Heart based on the Revelation of the Sacred Heart was rapidly spread by the Sisters of the Visitation Order and the priests of the Jesuits, not only in France but throughout the world.

"By 1688, a cathedral consecrated to the Sacred Heart of Jesus was built at Paray-le-Monial, and in 1765, Pope Clement XIII officially recognized the Revelation of the Sacred Heart. In 1856, Pope Pius IX established the Feast of the Sacred Heart of Jesus. In 1899, Pope Leo XIII published the encyclical letter *Annum Sacrum* and appealed for devotion to the Sacred Heart of Jesus. In 1900, he consecrated all of humankind to the Sacred Heart of Jesus. Finally, St. Margaret Mary was canonized as a saint by Pope Benedict XV in 1920. Thus, the little town of Paray-le-Monial, where the Revelation of the Sacred Heart took place, became a holy shrine which attracts many pilgrims. As you may know, a great many orders and missionaries devoted to the Sacred Heart of Jesus were established throughout the world."

"Thank you, Cardinal André." Cardinal Stewart led the applause.

The atmosphere at this meeting was less tense than the ones that preceded it. Everyone seemed to feel that the Cross Immolation Syndrome was not in opposition to Christianity, as they had initially feared, but rather was something that had as its intention the inspiration of Christianity. Many Catholics present at the meeting thought, just as Sister Theresa herself did, that this revelation from Jesus might be a modern version of the Revelation of the Sacred Heart.

In general, most Protestants do not recognize distinguishing certain people as saints or in individual revelation from Jesus. Thus, it was difficult for them accept Sister Theresa's vision as a modern version of the Revelation of the Sacred Heart of Jesus. Nevertheless, some thought that it might have some positive significance.

As for Father Yamamoto, he was relieved to have given the report to such a reception, but he thought that this meeting hadn't resolved everything. The cause of Sister Theresa's symptom of feeling nausea at seeing the cross still remained a mystery. This bothered him. No one dared mention it, but he sensed that the same strange phenomenon might continue to occur in the world and that something unexpected might develop from it.

Some suggested that the name "the Cross Immolation Syndrome" should be changed, but they decided to let it be for the time being and reconsider it later. In any case, the meeting ended peacefully, calling for further meetings if there were any more revelations or any new developments.

CHAPTER 4
The Revelation

The Revived Words of the Child Jesus

Sister Theresa's Struggles

November 2007; Kyoto

A few months had gone by since the interview between Sister Theresa and Father Yamamoto. Sister Theresa had certainly never expected to see Seiichi Yamamoto under such odd circumstances. She was perhaps more mentally prepared than Father Yamamoto had been, because she had been notified in advance that it was Father Yamamoto who was com-ing to interview her. She had worried whether she could have peace in her heart after seeing him again. Nevertheless, she was grateful that the meeting had been guided by God's love and grace to a much greater ex-tent than she had imagined possible.

Any anxiety she had about meeting Father Yamamoto again had van-ished completely. In fact, she found herself unexpectedly calm. She was relieved to find that her love for Jesus was deeper than she had thought. She couldn't deny feeling a touch of loneliness in the midst of her calm-ness, but nothing more than that. Her love for Jesus had begun to grow deeper after her meeting with Father Yamamoto.

She had adored and loved Jesus before, but she was no different from countless other Christians who loved and admired Jesus. Just as for the majority of Christians, Jesus for her was as sublime as God and was someone with whom she personally could not be emotionally involved. She had read in the biographies of saints how they adored Jesus as though he were a lover or husband, but that was something beyond her understanding. She had thought that it had nothing to do with her be-cause she was not a saint.

Now her relationship with Jesus was changing. Since Jesus had reap-peared to her and given her the revelation, "I have been misunderstood. I want you to understand my heart," a more adoring and more intimate emotion for Jesus, different from what she had felt before, was begin-ning to grow in her heart—a sweet emotional stimulus she had never experienced before.

Although she had such a feeling, she couldn't possibly believe that she was worthy or qualified to have a deep loving relationship such as the saints had with Jesus. At the same time, she noticed that there was something vague and indistinct in her heart which she wasn't comfortable with.

Is there anything wrong with how I feel about Father Yamamoto? She thought, but that didn't seem to be the problem. If there was any problem, she thought that it was with her relationship with Jesus.

Have I been thoughtless?

She questioned if having expressed her own opinion about what Jesus had told her was imprudent of her. But no matter how much she thought about it, she couldn't think that was the problem.

Have I said anything wrong?

She couldn't have said anything wrong. She tried to recall what she had been taught about Jesus' cross. According to the traditional Church doctrine, Jesus was predestined to be crucified, from the time of the Garden of Eden onward. Having disobeyed the commandment not to eat of the fruit of the Tree of the Knowledge of Good and Evil, the so-called "forbidden fruit", Adam and Eve's arrogance and disobedience was the first sin of humankind, the original sin, and it became the root of all the sins committed ever since. Adam and Eve were exiled from the Garden of Eden and as a result, humankind was destined to suffer and die. Humankind then multiplied the error, sinning repeatedly.

In spite of such faithlessness and sinfulness, the God of love desired to save humankind. However, saving all of humankind from sin was impossible for any sinful human being. It was only possible for God, who is sinless. God then planned to save humankind by sending His only Son as the second Adam and making him die in place of humankind, paying the price for their redemption. He chose the Israelites and guided them to prepare the way for God to send the Savior, the Messiah. The time came, and Jesus was sent to this world in order to bring eternal salvation by overcoming the physical death caused by Adam's sin through his physical death and resurrection. That was why Jesus inevitably had to be crucified.

This plan had been prophesied in verses such as those about "the suffering servant of the Lord" in Isaiah 53: "Yet it was our infirmities that he bore, our sufferings that he endured, while we thought of him as stricken, as one smitten by God and afflicted. But he was pierced for our offenses, crushed for our sins, upon him was the chastisement that makes us whole, by his stripes we were healed…the LORD laid upon him the guilt of us all. Oppressed and condemned, he was taken away. Though he had done no wrong nor spoken any falsehood...he shall take away the sins of many, and win pardon for their offenses."

This was what Sister Theresa had learned many times in church and in the convent about the death of Jesus on the cross. It was what the priests had told her, and what she had read in Christian books.

My interpretation of Jesus' heart cannot possibly be wrong, because this is not my own opinion. It is based on the most central teaching of the Church. Then what could be wrong? She wondered.

Still, there was that vague and indistinct sense of misgiving. She could not find the answer, no matter how much she thought about it.

When she thought of Jesus' solitary way of the cross, her heart broke in pain. Jesus was now saying, "Please understand my heart," because many people ignored his pain as they pursued their own happiness and material well-being. She earnestly wished to remove the misunderstanding and understand the sorrowful, solitary heart of Jesus, who had not been truly understood. She yearned to console him.

Sister Theresa was happy that her feelings of adoration for the cross were coming back to her again. She was enraptured in a sweet feeling for the cross and looked up at the cross in her room. Just then, that disgusting nausea attacked her again.

Why now? Could I be making a terrible mistake?

She collapsed in tears, horrified and riddled with anxiety, not knowing what made her so uneasy.

The Second Appearance

Three weeks after the first revelation, Jesus appeared to Sister Theresa again and asked her, "What do you think about my death on the cross?"

"I believe that your death on the cross was God's desire from the very beginning and therefore it was your desire."

"Do you think you understand my heart believing that?"

Sister Theresa wondered, "Why does Jesus ask such a question?" but she honestly replied, "Yes, I do."

Then Jesus said something she had never expected: "I want you to pray and think again."

She was surprised to hear these words from Jesus and could not grasp what he was trying to say. His words seemed to deny the fundamental Christian doctrine of the inevitability of the cross. She was riddled with doubt about this second revelation.

"Is this really Jesus? If he is really Jesus, he couldn't have told me to think over my words or position."

Feeling ashamed that she doubted, she asked Jesus with the intention of getting rid of the doubt, "Jesus, what do you mean by that? Wasn't the death on the cross God's desire and your desire from the beginning?"

"You must think about it yourself."

Jesus said this and left.

With an Open Mind Again

"What I have believed could be wrong."

When one begins to doubt something he or she has believed and treasured, that is a most serious and dangerous moment. At the same time, it can be a moment full of new possibilities, a time for conversion and progress.

What Jesus told Sister Theresa to do in the second revelation—to pray and discern if the cross was God's desire and therefore Jesus' desire was right or not—shocked her a great deal. This was a critical pass in her life that had the potential to completely overturn what had so far been the basis of her existence. The firm foundation on which she had stood all her life was now shaking violently.

It would have been much easier if it had been suggested to her by an atheist, or someone who was indifferent to or opposed to Jesus' teachings. In that case, all she would have to do would be to deny and resist it, praying that the deluded person would someday see the light. However, as far as she could discern, the revelation was given by Jesus himself. Her old defenses, security, and peace of mind that she was firmly within the teachings of the Church no longer stood firm.

She thought she should perhaps consult the director of the convent, Sister Hostia, or even Father Yamamoto, but Jesus had told her that she must think about it herself. Even he had not been willing to answer her directly. She thought that the only way left for her was to face the problem and question if what she had believed was really true or not, though it was a lonely, frightening, and difficult prospect fraught with the possibility that her life was going to be forever altered by the answers she found.

When she actually tried to question whether Jesus' death on the cross was God's desire or not, she felt stymied, overwhelmed by the seriousness the question. She was frightened, because questioning this seemed to chip away at the rock of faith Christianity had erected and treasured for two thousand years. She also thought that it was beyond her to deal with such a momentous question. Even just thinking about it seemed arrogant.

After struggling and struggling, she finally took a step forward. She would approach it in prayer. That way, she felt would be safe going beyond the boundaries of thought she had always observed. This was a very small step, but it was also a great big step, even to entertain the notion that everything she knew about Jesus up to this point had perhaps been mistaken. What finally pushed her forward was the thought that if Jesus' heart had been misunderstood, she wanted to truly understand him out of love. Surely she could not go far astray with that approach. She got up earlier than the other Sisters and spent time offering special prayers. She often meditated on Jesus' heart as he must have felt on his way to the cross, following the "the Stations of the Cross" in the convent yard.

"Please purify my heart and thoughts and let me think about Jesus' death on the cross correctly. Please guide me so that I can truly understand the heart of Jesus."

She prayed seriously, looking for a clue, but it was difficult. She struggled for days without finding a way, and one day her determination quaked. Then, suddenly, the words of Jesus, "What do you really think" came back to her mind.

Those words of Jesus made me feel as though what I thought were not my own thoughts and feelings but rather what I was taught to think. What does this mean?

As she thought about it in many different ways, she came to realize that her thoughts and the teaching of the Church were inseparable in her mind. They were so closely united within her that she could not tell the boundary between them; she could not tell how much of what she thought came from the teachings of the Church and how much was her own thoughts and beliefs.

Jesus asked me what I thought about his death on the cross. He may have wanted to tell me that what I had thought was my idea was not really mine, and that it was the teaching of the Church and that he wanted me to think about what I really feel about his death on the cross.

Come to think of it, I may have never questioned if Jesus' death on the cross was God's desire or not until Jesus told me to think about it. But why haven't I ever questioned it before?

Because it is treated as a self-evident fact and a major premise in Christianity. That is was probably why I never questioned it. But could we all have been wrong somehow?

Sister Theresa soon came to the conclusion that although she had totally accepted the teaching that Jesus' death on the cross was God's desire, she needed to get rid of that premise and have an open mind again and search for her own thoughts and feelings on the matter. When she realized this, she felt as if she saw a dim light shining far ahead of her where it had been completely dark before and nothing could be seen.

A New Relationship to the Cross

Although she saw a dim light, Sister Theresa still spent difficult days continuing to pray and search. Getting away from the preconceived idea that Jesus' death on the cross was God's desire and opening her mind to any other possibility was more difficult than she had expected it to be. Sister Theresa wanted to feel Jesus' death on the cross with her own heart. If she did so, she thought, it might affirm the age-old faith in a revolutionary way; perhaps that was the message and the reason why she was going through this. Yet, as long as she hoped for that outcome, she realized that her mind was still not open enough to a radical encounter with Jesus and the cross that might lead her up theological avenues she felt ill-prepared to explore.

She spent lonely and difficult days, but sometimes she felt that her journey was incredibly meaningful. These efforts were bringing her closer to Jesus' heart, and she believed that eventually she find herself loving Jesus more deeply and completely than ever before. That was worth some strain and doubt.

One evening she was struggling alone, pondering as she read the Holy Bible while sitting on a bench in the yard of the Sisters' home. Some children were playing with a ball near her. The ball accidentally rolled towards her. As she picked it up and tried to roll it back to them, she suddenly remembered clearly the incident in her childhood when she was five years old. The Child Jesus had come down from the statue of the Mother Mary and played with her, rolling a ball. The words of Jesus then, which she did not think were so important, came back to her mind now.

The Child Jesus had told her, "Let's pull out the cross, because it's not necessary."

She remembered that when he said it, he was very intense and somehow looked so lonely that it had worried her.

Was Jesus trying to tell me that his death on the cross was not necessary?

Sister Theresa quietly uttered this thought, but suddenly she became terribly anxious, thinking of the horrifying implications of that.

"That...that can't be possible. I must be thinking too much, because it can't possibly be true that the cross was not necessary. Without the cross, there is no resurrection, and that means that there is no salvation or redemption from human sin by the blood shed by Jesus. Without it, the two-thousand-year-old Christian history that began based on the cross and the resurrection couldn't have existed. The cross was inevitable and necessary for Christianity. Christianity is not Christianity without it.

She talked to herself so and tried dispel the horrible doubt she had just murmured.

At the same time, the Catholic Church had a strong sense of the tragedy of the cross; Good Friday commemorations vividly brought forth the horror of the fact that the Son of God was nailed to a piece of wood and died a tortuous death. On Good Fridays, an atmosphere of sorrow and horror at what humanity had done to the Son of God pervaded the Church—often aided by what seemed like uncannily bad weather. The Church celebrated not the death, but the resurrection. Was the Church onto something that it had never really articulated—the pervasive sorrow surrounding the ultimately triumphant cross? Or was she being a heretic—a madwoman? And why, of all people, was she able to converse with Jesus to such a degree that she had been visited by a representative from Rome who hoped that she had a key to the Cross Immolation Syndrome that was taking place all over the world?

She was not even sure she should be a nun any more. She was not sure she was still in her right mind.

The Tears of Jesus

The Very Person Who Misunderstood Jesus' Heart

The question, "Has Jesus been trying to tell me that the cross was unnecessary?" did not disappear from Sister Theresa's heart. The more she tried to get away from that burning question, the more it resounded in her brain.

"If the death of Jesus was not necessary, does it mean that there was a different purpose for his birth? But what else could it be, other than the redemption from sins by the death on the cross?" She had never imagined that there could be salvation any better than the redemption by Jesus' death on the cross and his resurrection.

"Jesus' cross and his resurrection are the only, absolute, ultimate salvation and there is no other true salvation. Jesus will come again at the end of this world to give the final judgment."

She had repeatedly heard this and had believed it. She had also taught this to children at Sunday schools. The thought that what she had believed to be true may have been wrong gave her extreme anxiety and confused her.

On the other hand, in the midst of such anxiety and confusion, when she thought, without prejudice, that it was possible that Jesus' cross was not inevitable and that it had not been planned by God, nor was it God's desire and that there may have been a different plan, every fragment of the strange incidents that she had experienced since her childhood seemed to come together.

It was as though the sun began to rise and clear the mist away and what was not visible before began to appear. Above all, when she thought, *The cross was not necessary,* she felt that she could solve the puzzle: *Why do I feel nausea seeing a cross?* She had been struggling because she had not been able to understand its meaning, no matter how many times she asked herself. Furthermore, this made her feel closer to what Jesus truly meant by the revelation "My heart has been misunderstood."

If Jesus had to go the way of the cross for some reason, although it was not the original desire of either God or Jesus, could there be any greater misunderstanding than this? It would mean that what Christianity had believed from its beginning was entirely the opposite of the true heart of Jesus.

Sister Theresa thought that perhaps this might be the answer to her prayer: "Please let me understand your true heart." However, her new insight threw her into the depths of struggles at the same time.

What have I done? I myself have not understood what Jesus has truly been feeling!

She had arrogantly thought that she understood Jesus' heart, but she had not. The fact that she had thought she understood his heart had deeply hurt Jesus and made him sad. When she discerned it, she was shocked and terrified at the graveness of her sin.

She was very ashamed of herself and, at the same time, she thought that she was a disgusting hypocrite. She was miserable. She could not forgive herself for being arrogant. Tears of sorrow and lamentation started to fall and would not stop. She spent days suffering, tormented by feelings of guilt. She did not know if there was any way to reach the other side of this pain.

One night, in the midst of her struggles, Sister Theresa had a dream.

In the dream, she entered a cathedral—the most beautiful cathedral she had ever seen. It was like a huge, golden, ornate ribcage with the altar like a vibrant heart. Everywhere there was a sense of life. Flowers seemed to nod at her, shouting colors of beauty and vitality. Velvet was draped everywhere. Golden light poured over the altar, lighting up the frescoes that would have rivaled the Sistine Chapel. Lifelike porcelain statues of saints, clothed in real silk, were mounted around the altar. Centrally located, where a cross or depiction of Jesus would normally rest, there was a throne of gold. The scrollwork was baroque and elaborate and the cushions, ample to the overflow, were covered in royal purple velvet.

As she gazed, Jesus appeared and walked toward the throne. He was wearing a long cape over a white silken robe. His sandals were of gold. The cape was made of beautiful white fur, flecked with specks of silver grey. On his head he wore a coronation crown with jewels that flashed almost blindingly, speaking of a spiritual power strong enough to direct the world.

Sister Theresa fell to her knees, overwhelmed with love for him and stunned by his splendor.

Jesus indicated the throne and said, "This is the throne of David."

She nodded.

"I was not to be King of Kings only in a spiritual sense. Look up Isaiah 9:7."

Sister Theresa woke up from the dream, memorizing the chapter and verse numbers Jesus had mentioned. Of course, she knew it was the famous quote from Isaiah:

"Of the increase of his government and of peace there shall be no end, upon the throne of David, and upon his kingdom to order it, and to establish it with judgment and with justice from henceforth even forever."

There had been nothing in the dream to indicate that the throne was anything but a real throne. Jesus was talking about a Kingdom of God on earth, administered by him.

She gleaned from the dream that he was to have been the literal King of Kings.

What Was God's Heart Regarding the Cross?

Sister Theresa struggled with her feelings of chagrin and guilt over having not understood her Jesus before. Then one day, Jesus appeared to Sister Theresa again. This was the third appearance outside of a dream. However, she felt so sad and sorry and ashamed that she could not raise her head.

"Sister Theresa, it's all right now. Raise your head," Jesus began to speak to her gently.

Sister Theresa slowly raised her head. Her face was swollen from crying.

"Was it totally a misunderstanding to believe that you came on earth in order to die on the cross?" she asked. "That your heart was lonely and pained by this? That you came to be accepted as the King of Kings here on earth as well as in heaven?"

"I see how you reproach yourself, but please understand that the problem you are struggling about is not simply your own but rather a problem that involves the entire Christian church. It is the essence of the Revelation of the True Heart, which I am revealing to you."

Sister Theresa shuddered at Jesus' words. As she steadied her breathing, however, she realized that she might never have such a precious chance to directly talk with Jesus again. Although she thought that it was presumptuous of her to do so, she dared to ask him again with courage:

"Why is it that you have never told it to anyone? I believe that you didn't say anything like that in the Revelation of the Sacred Heart to St. Margaret Mary Alacoque, whom our congregation respects in particular. Why didn't you reveal your true feelings then?"

"I tried to give the same message, but no one was able to understand it. It was because the message of a revelation is greatly influenced by the person who receives and interprets it and by the interpretation that the Church puts upon it."

"Does that mean you told St. Margaret Mary the same thing?"

"Of course, I tried to. I have tried to convey my true feelings not only to the Catholics but also to all Christians. God Our Father chose the people of Israel and guided them for a long period of time not for the purpose of persecuting and killing me, the Savior. It was so that they would believe in me and unite with me and establish the Kingdom of God in this world as well as in the spirit world. The dogma that it was God's desire and therefore my desire to be crucified and be killed has been such a big barrier. I was to live—and lead."

"But there are many verses written in various parts of the Bible that make us interpret your death on the cross as God's desire and that therefore it was inevitable for you to go the way of the cross."

"I did not write the Bible. My words are written in it, but things other than my own words are also included. What is written in the Bible already includes interpretations made by people.

"'The Kingdom of God is approaching. Repent and believe the Gospels.' This was what I said at the very beginning of my ministry. People at that time never thought of the Kingdom of God as only existing in the world after death. The Kingdom of God meant a Kingdom of God on earth, and that was what I meant. "

Sister Theresa was surprised that Jesus spoke to her much more than in his previous appearances. His next words surprised her even more.

"Sister Theresa, I did not call you so that you would reproach yourself for your sins and struggle. I want you to go tell what you have begun to understand about my heart to all the Christians and to all the people in the world. This is what I have called you for."

Hearing these words from Jesus, Sister Theresa was terrified.

"Jesus, I cannot possibly do such an extraordinary thing."

"It may not be possible with human ability, but if you really believe me and love me, there will definitely be a way."

These words of Jesus reminded her of when she had pulled out the cross from the ball of earth with the Child Jesus. She did not believe him then, and the Child Jesus told her to believe him. When she believed him and pulled with all her strength, with Jesus' help, the cross came off.

It seemed to her the situation then was completely different this time.

"Jesus, I really want to believe you, but such an extraordinary mission is too great a responsibility for me. Please give this mission to someone else who has more knowledge in the Bible and theology and a more respectable position. It's impossible for me."

It would have been more understandable if it had been in a country with a Christian foundation, but she could not comprehend why Jesus would give such an important mission to a nameless Sister in Japan, where only less than one percent of the total population was Christian. What influence could she possibly have? She thought that Jesus would be more easily accepted by many Christians if he appeared to a cardinal or an archbishop in a Christian country that could influence the entire Christian church, or perhaps to a famous theologian whose thoughts were already accepted worldwide, or to the superior of a large monastery, or to the Roman Pope.

"It is not for you to decide whether it is impossible for you or not. The most important thing is not knowledge of the Bible or theology, nor one's abilities and social status. The most precious thing is love and whether one really understands my heart or not. If you truly understand my heart and can truly love me, this will indeed be a power stronger than any other. I am with a person who truly loves me. I have chosen you, who is nameless and the most humble, in order to reveal that love is superior to everything."

Sister Theresa was stunned to know that Jesus seriously wanted her to accomplish this mission. At the same time, she was moved in her heart, feeling Jesus' desperation to be understood. She remembered the time when the Child Jesus asked her to remove the cross because it was too heavy. She also remembered how sorry she felt because the cross was so heavy and how happy Jesus looked when he had his cross taken off.

"You now know my heart more than anyone else through the Revelation of the True Heart, don't you? That is indeed the greatest grace you have ever received."

"Yes, it is so. The true feelings of Jesus, which nobody knew or imagined, have been revealed to me, and I know that Jesus himself has told it to me. This may be the answer to what I have been praying for."

"Yes. That's right. You must not forget that this is the most precious treasure you have, and that it is a source of strength capable of helping you overcome any difficulty."

Jesus spoke as if he could see through Sister Theresa's heart.

"Then what must I do? Even if I tell people what you have told me, no one will believe that it is the truth."

"I will send Father Yamamoto as your assistant. He will support you. I was with Father Yamamoto's father when he had lung cancer surgery."

She did not know anything about the lung cancer surgery of Father Yamamoto's father. Neither did she know what that had to do with this. However, she was very surprised and at the same time happy to hear Father Yamamoto's name mentioned by Jesus. These words of Jesus expressed that Jesus knew every step of her life and had accepted and forgiven everything.

"How deeply Jesus knows me!"

Of course, she knew that Jesus knew everything about human beings, but she was indescribably overwhelmed to hear things in detail.

However, even after hearing all this from Jesus, she felt that there was something in her mind that prevented her from making a firm decision. She thought that it might have something to do with her background as an abandoned child, but she wasn't sure what exactly the problem was. She had thought that it had been resolved when she reencountered Jesus after all those years, but something still bothered her.

The words of Jesus about her, calling her a "nameless and most humble person" and her background of having been abandoned as a child wouldn't link together in her mind. She was hesitant, not knowing how to express herself.

Then Jesus surprised her by saying, "You have greatly suffered because you were abandoned by your parents. For you, being an abandoned child meant that you were a sinner and unworthy, which made you suffer even more. In fact, I chose you because of this, because of that which you have suffered most about."

"I don't understand."

"Sister Theresa, the struggles you have gone through as an abandoned child were my own struggles. No one knows that I suffered loneliness and bitterness as an illegitimate child. You can understand the pain I had in my heart as a lonely child."

Meeting Jesus had been full of surprises, but nothing shocked her more than these words.

"How can that be possible? Jesus is the only son of God and was raised without any problems by the Virgin Mary and St. Joseph, his foster father, in a holy family with divine love."

"It's natural that you don't understand what I am saying. During the last two thousand years, Christians have put me in the position of God and emphasized my divinity and have hardly shown interest in my struggles as a human being. If you read the Bible carefully, you should be able to know that I am telling you the truth."

"I had never thought that what I had suffered the most about would be the key to understanding your heart," she said in wonder.

There were many things St. Theresa still couldn't understand, but she felt the mystery of salvation through God's love and felt that something was resolved. She could not find any more words to say to Jesus. Although she was still very anxious whether she could do such a bold thing as to proclaim what she had learned from Jesus, she thought there was no other way but to believe and obey.

"Jesus, I deeply thank you for having guided me and for revealing your precious heart to me. Please forgive me for arrogantly thinking that I had understood your heart before this. How repeatedly have I crucified you because of it! How many times have I whipped you, given you a crown of thorns, and nailed your hands and feet on the cross and pierced your side.

But now, you have revealed to me your true heart. For the last two thousand years, all the Christians, including myself, have believed that you had wished to be crucified and die from the very beginning. What a cruel thing we have been doing to you!"

As she said this to Jesus, her heart was breaking, feeling the graveness of her sin and even more the pain of Jesus' misunderstood heart. Tears rolled down her cheeks. In tears, she vowed firmly in her heart, "I believe what Jesus has told me, and I will offer the rest of my life to telling people about the true heart of Jesus, no matter how impossible it may seem or how difficult it may be."

When she determined to do so, she suddenly felt something warm touch her forehead. Surprisingly, it was drops of tears falling from Jesus' eyes.

"Your tears are very precious to me," he told her.

She was deeply moved in her heart to find that her thoughts unexpectedly brought tears from Jesus. It was a sweet sensation that she had never experienced before, as though her heart had touched Jesus' heart. Treasuring this, she thought that she could endure any difficulty. She wanted to be infinitely immersed in this supreme bliss.

Chapter 5
Determination

The Given Mission

Busy Days

January 2008; Kyoto

The reunion with Sister Theresa had been a significant event for Father Yamamoto. Her unexpected words and generous attitude had liberated him from the struggles he'd had for a long period of time. Nevertheless, Father Yamamoto was too busy with his work to give it much thought.

The investigation of the Cross Immolation Syndrome was a very important responsibility, but in terms of the time he spent, it was a mere portion of all the work he had to do. The major work of Father Yamamoto was that of a Catholic priest. It involved not only the work within the church he was responsible for but also looking after college students of the entire Kansai Second Parish and the work of the Japanese Catholic Church.

Some of the work he was responsible for was offering Mass every morning at the monastery for Sisters, giving Saturday and Sunday Masses at his church, anointing the sick and visiting those who could not come to church, conducting wedding ceremonies and funerals, teaching catechism and faith to those who were preparing to receive the Sacraments. He worked during major church events such as Christmas and Easter, helped at bazaars and various meetings, and did consultation and counseling.

He had such a busy schedule that it almost made him feel as if he had been in Rome many years ago. Yet no matter how busy he was, he felt valuable and joyful at being able to work as a priest back in Japan.

Because of declining numbers of people seeking the priesthood, the Church has given many of the responsibilities of priests to lay people, but priests still had a lot of work to do. The church had enough work looking after the present members and guiding them. But in addition to this, it had another important mission of evangelizing people who still did not know Christianity. In Japan, the Christian population was very small and the missionary work was difficult. There were many issues to deal with. There was an almost infinite amount of work to do.

His three and a half years of studying abroad had given him impetus. Those who have studied in Rome frequently become bishops, and while there are priests who become bishops without having studied in Rome, many candidates for bishop go to Rome to study. However, for Father Yamamoto, studying in Rome was not necessarily preparation to become a bishop in the future; it was a useful experience for working as an ordinary priest. Still, he was not sure how much of the theology that he had studied in Rome would directly help him in his busy daily work as a priest. What the lay members and others who come to the church were seeking was not academic knowledge or complex theology. They were looking for actual help, love, consolation, and the sense of being saved.

Father Yamamoto belonged to a parish supervised by a bishop, yet not attached to a monastery such as the Jesuits, the Franciscans, the Maryknolls, or the Paris Missions. Father Yamamoto was a parish priest, in contrast to a monastery priest. The vow of lifelong celibacy was the same, but monastery priests take an additional vow of "honest poverty" and do not hold any private property, whereas parish priests are allowed to have private possessions.

Since priests do not have families of their own, they do not need much property. Of course, some priests save up money. After the death of such priests, the parish generally inherits the money, as they leave no heirs. Many save just enough to cover their funeral expenses so that it won't be a financial burden on the parish when they die. However, the church provides for those who do not have such money saved up for their own funerals.

No matter how hard they worked, the priests wouldn't receive a raise it or be promoted to a higher rank, except for some special priests. Nevertheless, they worked in order to build their treasure of invisible riches in heaven. Their treasures would be how much they loved God and others. That is why their spiritual interaction with God and heartfelt exchanges with people nourished their hearts.

Indeed, there are some who are priests in name only who are criticized for having become school teachers, owners of institutions for the handicapped, or social activists. There are some who secretly have a relationship with a woman or a man. Furthermore, there are some who seem to value their hobbies more than their work in the church.

In fact, an Italian Bishop who studied with Father Yamamoto in Rome complained that one of the parish priests in his parish started to raise domestic animals and was almost more like a farmer than a priest. The church members ceaselessly complained that taking care of his animals was more important for him than his church work. Yet Father Yamamoto believed that the majority of priests still worked for God and the people.

Priests take a vow at their ordination that their bishop is their superior at work and at the same time he is somewhat like their father. For Father Yamamoto, Bishop Hayata is a very reliable person in that respect. Priests are bound together by an invisible thread. It is probably because they naturally respect and sympathize with each other for making effort and struggling to answer the call from God to become a priest—a very difficult vocation.

Father Yamamoto had some friends who were priests and whom he could trust. Sometimes he met them. However, he never told them about the Cross Immolation Syndrome or about the revelation Sister Theresa claimed to have received. He did, however, tell Bishop Hayata.

Although Father Yamamoto was busy, his reunion with Sister Theresa and the revelation of Jesus she told him about remained in the back of his mind. Of course, he had the responsibility to report back to the committee for the Cross Immolation Syndrome, and that was important. He was even more serious in his handling of this case because he had once been close to Sister Theresa in his youth.

That was why he continued looking into it in his own way, even after making his report to the committee. However, the words, "My heart has been misunderstood. I want you to understand my heart" were not enough to go on to make any judgments, and he thought that it was still too early to draw any conclusions. He somehow felt he had not heard the end of it, and this feeling intensified day by day.

The Revelation of the True Heart of Jesus

About five months after their first interview, Sister Hostia, the director of the Congregation of Consolation of the Sacred Heart of Jesus, contacted Father Yamamoto again.

"Sister Theresa says that she has received another message from Jesus."

It was already a new year. A few days later, Father Yamamoto visited the convent.

It was a cold but sunny day. The plum blossoms in the garden of the convent were beginning to bloom. Just as at the previous interview, Sister Hostia welcomed him warmly and led him into the reception room. She did not talk much this time and left the room right away.

"Thank you for giving me your precious time. You must be busy," said Sister Theresa in an apologetic manner. She heard from Sister Hostia that he had been busy working.

"This is my work, so you don't have to worry." Father Yamamoto was happy that he was able to talk with her in a natural way. "Now will you tell me the message of the new revelation?"

"Father, I'm honestly very worried that no one will believe the message."

"Does that mean that the message this time contains astonishing content?"

"Yes, I think so."

Father Yamamoto looked a little tense.

"If it is a revelation from Jesus, let's trust that Jesus will guide us," he said cautiously yet with confidence.

She was still anxious, but these words of Father Yamamoto helped her calm down. Trusting the words of Jesus promising her to send Father Yamamoto to assist her, she gathered the courage to speak.

She began to tell him about her struggles and some incidents after the first revelation, about the second revelation and the happenings that followed it and Jesus' words saying, that the death on the cross was neither God's nor Jesus' desire but was the result of the people's disbelief in him. This was the core of the new revelation from Jesus. She also told him about her dream and her conversation with Jesus.

She explained that her background as an abandoned child made Jesus feel that she could understand his heart better because he had spent a lonely childhood as an illegitimate child. She could not tell what Father Yamamoto was feeling from his facial expression, but she sensed that he was seriously listening to her.

After she finished speaking, Father Yamamoto was silent for a while. It wasn't actually such a long time, but it seemed like a very long time to Sister Theresa.

Meantime, she desperately prayed in her heart, "Please guide Father Yamamoto so that he will accept the message of Jesus' revelation." This was natural, considering that Father Yamamoto's acceptance or lack of acceptance would have a decisive effect on her ability to accomplish the mission given to her by Jesus.

After a moment, Father Yamamoto began to speak.

"Is the new revelation saying that Jesus' words, 'I have been misunderstood. I want you to understand my true heart,' meant that although being crucified was neither God's desire nor his, it had been believed so?

Is this the misunderstanding that pains him?"

"Yes, I think that is the case."

"Then that means that Jesus had a different mission to accomplish, without dying, and if he had accomplished it, he could have brought a salvation greater than the salvation given by his death and resurrection on the cross. Does that mission mean establishing the Kingdom of God on this earth?"

"Yes, I think so."

Father Yamamoto was unexpectedly calm. She had anticipated that Father Yamamoto would react to her words and reject what she had to say, and that it would take him long to accept it, if he ever did. She was happy that his response was contrary to her expectations. She began to feel that Jesus' words, "I will send you Father Yamamoto to assist you," could really come true.

Father Yamamoto continued, "I find it strange that this revelation has a character quite different from other previous revelations of Jesus or of Mother Mary. Most of the previous revelations I know of contained warnings that said that if the message was not accepted, there would be a war, or some judgment would be given. This 'Revelation of the True Heart' from Jesus contains a revolutionary message that could fundamentally turn over traditional Christian interpretations. We can say that it has a content that can't possibly be accepted by church leaders and members who value the traditional interpretation. The message regarding how Jesus suffered as an illegitimate child or that Jesus' death on the cross was not inevitable and that it was not God's desire all seem utterly against the Christian faith, but in a sense they share some things common with the research results of modern theologians searching for the true historical image of Jesus.

"What I've heard from you is not so extremely far from what I believe and is not so difficult to believe. It's even amazing that what has been studied and discussed separately is unified in the view that the death of Jesus on the cross was not God's desire and that it was not inevitable. It is strange that nobody has been able to think that way until now—it seems a logical inquiry to pursue. Yet I must be honest and tell you that I still find it rather difficult to totally accept that this was revealed in the form of personal revelation to you."

"I understand that very well. But what you have just said has given me some hope."

"I must tell you one thing so that you won't misunderstand me. I don't find it so extraordinary, but this doesn't mean at all that the Church will easily accept the message of this revelation. Rather, I can't possibly believe that the Church would easily accept this as Jesus' revelation. My responsibility is only to report what I hear from you, and I am not in any position to convince the Church to accept it. I do not have the capacity to convince the Church."

Sister Theresa felt a sense of rejection from Father Yamamoto as he uttered these words, and she became uneasy. Yet the fact that Father Yamamoto was not denying the Revelation of the True Heart of Jesus as she had anticipated he might meant a great deal to Sister Theresa.

If he realizes his mission, there should be a way, she thought. For that to happen, she had to tell him what Jesus had told her about him.

"Will Father Yamamoto accept what Jesus said about him?"

Sister Theresa waited tensely.

"What?" Father Yamamoto asked in astonishment.

"Father Yamamoto, Jesus mentioned you in the revelation. May I talk about that now?" Sister Theresa said this with courage, hoping that he would calmly accept this too.

"What? Are you serious?"

Father Yamamoto, who had been calm, was now astonished and incredulous.

"When I repeatedly refused Jesus, saying I could not do such an outrageous thing as tell all Christians about the Revelation of the True Heart of Jesus, Jesus said, 'I will send you Father Yamamoto as your assistant. He will support you.'"

Father Yamamoto was totally at a loss. He had never imagined this would directly involve him. He had the responsibility to report to the committee and indeed he felt some personal interest in Sister Theresa and more interest in the Cross Immolation Syndrome than before because it involved her. Yet he had kept the position of an objective observer and considered none of it his responsibility. The moment he heard these words from her, his objectivity began to waver.

Father Yamamoto never dreamed he could do such an outrageous thing as try to bear this message as a revelation to other Christians. It was not that he was unsympathetic to some parts of the revelation. He was rather moved by it, in fact. But that didn't mean that he totally believed it came from Jesus himself. What was more, he couldn't possibly imagine that he had the responsibility to tell the message of the revelation to all Christians. He didn't think that Sister Theresa was making it up about

Jesus speaking to her about him, but he found it difficult to make himself believe that it was actually true.

"Did Jesus say anything else besides this?" he questioned her.

"He told me something about your father."

"What was that?"

"He said, 'I was with Father Yamamoto's father, Chuichi, when he had the lung cancer surgery.'"

Father Yamamoto was stunned. He had never mentioned his father, his father's name, or his surgery to Sister Theresa. She couldn't have known about it.

"Are you telling me this to enable me to discern that this revelation is from Jesus?"

He felt that there might be a deeper meaning to it. He thought that he might be able to find something about it if he knew more in detail about his father's surgery, but his father had died a few years before and he thought there was little hope of that.

When he put himself in Sister Theresa's position, he could well understand that her encounter with Jesus was deeply linked with her own consolation. He was personally happy about it. He could understand well that she must have experienced sorrow and bitterness over having been abandoned as a child. For her, it had to be true that the message of the revelation came from Jesus himself, and nothing could be greater for her than seeing it accepted by the Church.

However, if he had to assist her accomplish this mission that was another thing entirely. That was not a small responsibility he could fulfill with mere sympathy. In order to recognize it as his own responsibility, he needed to see it as his own vital calling.

Father Yamamoto sensed that these words of Jesus about him held some clue, but he hardly knew what it really had to do with him or what his real role was according to Jesus' revelation.

"I'm sorry," he said to Sister Theresa. "But I need to pray and try to sort things out. Please give me some time."

Father Yamamoto's sincerity was unmistakable. Sister Theresa could well understand the difficulty Father Yamamoto was facing. She had fulfilled her responsibility of telling him what she had to tell him, and now all she could do was to leave the rest to Father Yamamoto and Jesus.

"I thank you from the bottom of my heart for seriously and sincerely listening to what I said to you," she said gratefully.

Thus, their second interview ended.

The Connected Line

The Words of Janos Gago

Two weeks had passed since his second interview with St. Theresa. Meanwhile Father Yamamoto pondered on the words of Jesus she had reported to him that he was to be Sister Theresa's assistant. He had no other way to interpret this than that he was to assist her in her mission of telling the entire Christian church "the Revelation of the True Heart of Jesus".

Certainly, he had more knowledge in theology than Sister Theresa, but there were countless theologians in the world that he could not compare to. His knowledge of theology was inadequate to assist her.

Nevertheless, not only Catholics but also representatives of major Christian denominations from around the world had gathered to attend the committee about the Cross Immolation Syndrome, and having a position there to give a report about Sister Theresa would certainly give him a platform to fulfill the mission of telling all Christians about this new revelation.

However, accomplishing the mission didn't simply mean telling them about it. It meant persuading them that the revelation was actually from Jesus. When he thought in such a way, he recognized what he could do as an assistant, but the biggest problem was that he couldn't be as certain as Sister Theresa was that the revelation really came from Jesus himself.

"How can I know?" he wondered.

One day he came across a clue in an unexpected way. It was when he was reading a book by psychologist Carl Jung.

He was surprised as he read that the meaningless words repeated by a schizophrenic patient turned out to be a verse in the text of an ancient Egyptian religion called Mithraism, which had existed several thousand years ago. The patient, of course, had no knowledge of Mithraism or the Egyptian language. This case later became the basis for Jung to propose that, in addition to a personal unconscious, there was a collective unconscious in the human mind which connected people beyond time and distance.

"Do the words of Janos Gago who painted out the cross have any meaning?"

He immediately decided to contact Father Johann Schillebeeckx, a Dutch priest who had studied with him in Rome, who was also a member of the committee on the Cross Immolation Syndrome. Father Schillebeeckx excelled in ancient languages.

A week later, Father Yamamoto's notebook PC rang loudly. It was a Skype phone call from Johann.

"Seiichi, don't be surprised to hear this."

"What is it?"

"Your prediction was right."

"What do you mean?"

"The words of Janos Gago were not meaningless. Just as you had predicted, they had a meaning."

"Ah! Just as I thought! What language was he was speaking?"

"He was speaking in Aramaic, a dialect of Hebrew, the same language Jesus spoke," Johann' tone was serious. Although Father Yamamoto had expected to hear this, he was extremely excited.

"What on earth was he saying?"

"*La atit haka al gav de-tsaliv*, which means 'I did not come to die on the cross.'"

"'I did not come to die on the cross.'"

He thanked Johann and took his headset off. This meant a great deal to him. Thus, in addition to the fact that Sister Theresa knew about Chuichi's surgery, the words of Janos Gago, which had been thought to be gibberish, made Father Yamamoto think that the 'Revelation of the True Heart of Jesus' might have come from Jesus himself.

The Dream of Seiichi's Father

There was another thing that had been on Father Yamamoto's mind. It was the words of Jesus regarding his father, Chuichi:

"I was also with Father Yamamoto's father when he had his lung cancer surgery."

This had great significance because it meant that whoever Sister Theresa had been talking to spiritually knew something that Sister Theresa did not. This also convinced Father Yamamoto that she might indeed have been speaking to Jesus. However, Father Yamamoto wanted to investigate further. He went to visit Father Minamida in hopes of finding out more from him about when his father had his surgery. Father Minamida had taught the Catholic catechism to Chuichi and baptized him; he had also had a decisive influence on Seiichi becoming a priest.

Father Yamamoto first asked Father Minamida not to question why he was visiting him, but to tell him about his father's lung cancer surgery. Father Minamida was surprised, but he sensed from Father Yamamoto's demeanor that there might be a serious reason for this request, and he gladly agreed.

Father Yamamoto already knew most of what Father Minamida told him. There was only one thing Seiichi did not know. It was about the dream Chuichi had while he was unconscious after the surgery. Father Minamida told him the words Jesus had spoken to Chuichi in his dream:

"Search for my true heart, and I shall always be with you and your family."

When Father Yamamoto heard these words, fragments of things that had happened separately in his heart in the past suddenly were connected into a line. Jesus had not only prepared Sister Theresa, he had prepared Father Yamamoto too.

What had previously been Sister Theresa's dilemma was now Father Yamamoto's dilemma. He could no longer be an observer or a third person. This meant that he was to take the great responsibility of telling all Christians about "the Revelation of the True Heart of Jesus".

"Search for my heart."

Jesus' words, spoken to Chuichi some thirty years ago, were similar to the revelation given to Sister Theresa. The two were clearly linked and had a new and different meaning than he would have ever thought.

Father Yamamoto prayed to Jesus that he could adequately fulfill the difficult mission of assisting Sister Theresa.

The Death of the Pope and the Election of a New Pope

It was some time after Father Yamamoto had made a firm decision to accept the mission that he found out that the Pope died. The Pope had been loved by the people for a long period of time, and his death brought deep sorrow to the Italian people and to all Catholics throughout the world. He died from a complication of pneumonia. People knew that he had been suffering from kidney failure in his later years. Perhaps this had prepared them for his death. He was seventy-nine years old.

Cardinal Rahner, who was the head cardinal, the dean of the College of Cardinals, was trusted deeply by the late Pope. He was immediately appointed as the chairman of the funeral committee and busily prepared for the Pope's funeral service.

It was a grand funeral service. Kings, presidents, and prime ministers as well as Catholics from all over the world gathered to attend. The attendants were struck by the great influence of the Pope in the world.

The funeral was peacefully conducted. With no time to rest, Cardinal Rahner now had to take on the important responsibility of electing the new Pope. A few days after the nine days of mourning, during which the entire Vatican mourned, a "conclave"—an election by the Cardinals to choose the next Pope—was convened. "Conclave" literally means "to lock". All the people in the world were watching the chimney of the Sistine Chapel on TV to find out when the new Pope was elected. Black smoke, a sign that none of the candidates had obtained two thirds of the votes, had been coming out for days. On the sixteenth day, white smoke came out. It meant that a new Pope was elected. The church bells rang out loudly in celebration. Cardinal Hans Rahner was elected the new Pope.

He was crowned Pax I. Most of the conservative believers welcomed Cardinal Rahner as the new Pope. Many radical Catholics, however, who were seeking to reform the Catholic Church, were not satisfied with the result of this election.

Father Yamamoto honestly didn't know how to react to the coronation of Cardinal Rahner. It was Rahner who had created the negative name "The Cross Immolation Syndrome", and who had feared that the phenomena surrounding this syndrome were a threat against the entire Christian church. What would his election mean for Father Yamamoto and Sister Theresa' mission?

Cardinal Rahner had not given his personal opinion regarding the revelation of Jesus to Sister Theresa. Yet Father Yamamoto didn't dare think that he had changed his initial negative view. This could make the situation extremely difficult.

Father Yamamoto had taken a theology class from Cardinal Rahner and had visited him a few times in his office to ask questions. It was also Cardinal Rahner who had appointed Father Yamamoto to investigate Sister Theresa. He did know him personally; that might have great significance, considering his mission. It might not be totally impossible to see him personally. Father Yamamoto was trying to find some slight hope.

CHAPTER 6
Tension

Visiting the Land of Faith in the Sacred Heart

The Chapel of the Appearance of Jesus

March 2008; Paray-le-Monial, France.

Father Yamamoto was going to give his second report at the third meeting of the Committee for the Cross Immolation Syndrome. He took advantage of this opportunity and left earlier than his original plan to visit Paray-le-Monial in France: the origin of the devotion to the Sacred Heart—a place he had always wanted to visit. There is a monastery there where Jesus had appeared to St. Margaret Mary and had given the Revelation of the Sacred Heart in the 17th century.

He had begun to believe that "the Revelation of the True Heart of Jesus" came from Jesus himself, yet in order to tell this to Christians, there still was a problem he had to resolve. It had to do with the answer Jesus gave to Sister Theresa in response to her question, "Did you tell St. Margaret Mary the same thing you told me?" Jesus had said, "Of course, I tried to."

That meant that Jesus had also tried to tell St. Margaret Mary that his death on the cross was not God's desire.

"The Revelation of the Sacred Heart" and "the Revelation of the True Heart of Jesus" were both revelations concerning Jesus' heart. How were they intertwined? They seemed opposite in content.

"The Revelation of the Sacred Heart" focused on Jesus' death on the cross. It seemed to emphasize that his death on the cross was God's desire and that it was inevitable.

It was difficult for Father Yamamoto to believe that a revelation with the same message could be interpreted in completely opposite ways, depending on the person who received it. As Jesus had mentioned to Sister Theresa, if revelations were influenced by the person who interpreted them and by the Church's view of faith and Jesus, what did that say about the thinking of people at the time of the Revelation of the Sacred Heart?

If he didn't resolve this contradiction, he himself would not be fully convinced of "the Revelation of the True Heart of Jesus". Although he wasn't certain what he would find at Paray-le-Monial, he thought that he might be able to find some connection between the Revelation of the Sacred Heart and "the Revelation of the True Heart of Jesus".

The Revelation of the Sacred Heart was not as important for Christian denominations other than the Catholic Church. Even if he proved a link, he was not sure how theologically or theoretically persuasive that would be to other Christians. Yet sometimes faith went beyond theory or theology. Thus, he thought that the Revelation of the Sacred Heart might have great significance to his mission.

Father Yamamoto got permission to go to Paray-le-Monial from Bishop Hayata, and he arrived in Rome one week earlier than the committee meeting in order to do so. He left his luggage in Rome, visited a friend in Paris, and then left for Paray-le-Monial.

Paray-le-Monial is a small town located in Burgundy in the central part of France. Father Yamamoto parted from his friend and got on the TGV, the French bullet train, at the Lyon station in Paris. He got off just before Lyon and changed to a bus that went directly to Paray-le-Monial. It was faster than he had expected, and he arrived at the Paray-le-Monial Station two and a half hours after he left Paris. There were many old buildings in that section of the city and it seemed to look as it had in the 17th century.

St. Margaret Mary and St. Columbiere used to walk this road, he thought in wonderment.

It was early spring, and the night breeze felt soothing and comfortable to walk about in as he went to his lodgings for the night.

I Want to Know the Heart of Jesus

He woke up early the next day. When he opened the window, he saw a scene in a mist that reminded him of a medieval town with stone brick walls surrounding churches and old buildings that looked like palaces. He almost lost his sense of time. The place he was staying at was run by a monastery for Sisters. He offered "the prayer of the church" alone in the chapel and said a Mass and then had breakfast. There were some people staying there too, but not as many as he had expected.

He visited the Chapel of the Appearance and the Basilica of the Sacred Heart and some other places. On the facade of the Chapel of the Appearance, a painting of Jesus' appearance is painted with orange as its base color. This basilica was built as an extension after Jesus' apparition and was connected to the convent at the right side of the altar. The body of St. Margaret Mary was placed at the small altar in the right side of the chapel.

Father Yamamoto sat on a bench in the chapel and opened *The Autobiography of St. Margaret Mary*, a Japanese paperback book he had brought with him. He had read it before many years ago. He had not been able to finish reading it then, because the world it described was too remote from his. He never had a dream or vision of Jesus. But now, it had much to do with his problems, and he thought that if he read it there, he might be able to understand more.

He visited some other churches and convents as well and walked down the road on the riverside with trees along it, gazing at the Basilica of the Sacred Heart. Because it was such a small town, he walked the same places many times, going back and forth.

On the fourth morning, the day before he had to leave, Father Yamamoto felt full of complexity. He was thinking of giving up, yet at the same time he still felt pressured to find something here, some clue to unlock his puzzlement.

Father Yamamoto was struggling because if "the Revelation of the True Heart of Jesus" which Jesus revealed to Sister Theresa was true, and if it was true that Jesus didn't wish to die on the cross but rather wished to live and establish a Kingdom of God in this world, he couldn't understand why the revelation that St. Margaret Mary was given contradicted this and why it was accepted by Catholic authority and by so many people.

"Could one of the two revelations be right and the other wrong?" he wondered. "If both revelations are from Jesus, it would mean that St. Margaret Mary didn't correctly interpret what Jesus told her. I think it's impossible to prove that. Conversely, is it possible that Jesus' revelation to Sister Theresa, the words of Janos Gago, and Jesus saying that he knew about my father's surgery all weren't true and didn't come from Jesus?"

He didn't know how he was going to figure all this out.

After reading how St. Margaret Mary kissed human waste and even put such in her mouth to express her love for Jesus or to express self-denial, he thought that he couldn't possibly go so far as she had gone in faith. This shook his determination to clarify the contradiction between the Revelation of the Sacred Heart and the Revelation of the True Heart of Jesus.

He would have given up by now, but he felt something was changing in his heart. He was beginning to feel in a way he had never felt before, as if Jesus knew and sympathized with his search.

Father Yamamoto had never seriously thought about Jesus' heart until he came to know The Revelation of the True Heart. Now he wanted to know the true heart of Jesus. He was happy to have such a desire. As it deepened, he realized that it was natural as a Christian to wish to know the true heart of Jesus. He thus realized that he didn't need to think that he was unqualified or that it would be presumptuous to wish for it.

"It was worth coming here just to be able feel this way," he said to himself.

So he thought as he walked slowly down the street from the Basilica to the convent in the dusk.

Jesus Wished the Disciples to Stay Awake and Pray with Him

Finally, it was the fifth day, his last day in Paray-le-Monial. After finishing his breakfast, Father Yamamoto left the convent with his luggage. He didn't have much time before the bus departed, but he wanted stop by the Chapel of the Appearance one last time before heading for the station. He walked very fast, almost running, to the chapel.

It was raining. There was a child begging at the front door. When he tried to take some change from his pocket to give to the child, *The Autobiography of St. Margaret Mary* fell out. He had finished reading the whole book during his stay, but he hadn't discovered anything in regard to his own dilemma. The autobiography gave him the impression that it consciously or unconsciously modified Jesus' revelation, but he thought that it would be impossible to prove that. Yet he had not given up on finding some clues within it, and he kept it in his pocket to read again on the train to Paris. After giving some change to the child, he picked up the book and found it was mud-stained. He wiped the page with tissues and put it back in his pocket. He then took out his umbrella, held it over the child, and told the child to keep it. Then he went inside to pray.

"Jesus, I came here to visit Paray-le-Monial in search for your true heart, and I spent four days in prayers and meditation. I was not able to find what I was looking for, but this place has become very dear to me.

I have found something very precious by coming here, which gives me a mysterious peace of mind. This is a grace more valuable than anything else. I deeply thank you.

"I must now head for Rome and give a report to the committee on the Cross Immolation Syndrome. I entrust myself totally to you, so please guide me."

Father Yamamoto finished praying, left the chapel, and hurried to the station. When he looked back, the child he had met earlier was waving at him, which made Father Yamamoto smile. On his way to the station, he remembered each day he spent in Paray-le-Monial, and each and every place he had visited was lodged in his mind and heart as a sweet memory.

"Do I long for them so much because I spent the time there with Jesus?"

As he watched the scenery of Paray-le-Monial passing by in the bus window, he suddenly remembered the child. He thought of something and caught his breath. Father Yamamoto took out the autobiography from the pocket of his coat and searched for the mud-stained page. It was the page where Jesus was speaking to St. Margaret Mary about when Jesus had just finished his last supper and was about to pray with his disciples for the final time in the Garden of Gethsemane.

Jesus had told his disciples to stay awake and pray with him in the Garden of Gethsemane, but they all fell asleep. Immediately after that, Jesus was caught, tried, and crucified.

Jesus' desire regarding this issue was written in St. Margaret Mary's autobiography. Jesus wanted her to stay awake on Thursday nights from eleven to midnight in order to comfort the pain he suffered from being abandoned by his disciples as he prayed in the Garden of Gethsemane.

This is called the "the duty of the Holy Hour", which has been kept in convents since then. He remembered hearing from Sister Theresa that the Congregation of the Consolation of the Sacred Heart of Jesus, which Sister Theresa belonged to, also kept this hour. He didn't think it was so important then, but now he thought that it had an extremely important meaning.

Father Yamamoto tried to recall what Sister Theresa said about the "duty of the Holy Hour".

"Other congregations have also kept 'the duty of the Holy Hour,' but our congregation, in particular, has kept it strictly. When I was still a child, I used to sleep in a big room with other children. We were supposed to go to bed at eight. The Sisters used to take turns to make a round to check and see if we were asleep or not. But, for some reason, on Thursday nights, all the Sisters disappeared somewhere between eleven and midnight. We children could get up at eleven and enjoy ourselves as much as we wanted until midnight, while the Sisters were all gone.

"After I grew up and became an adult, I joined the convent to become a Sister and participated in the prayer to keep 'the Holy Hour'. Then I learned for the first time why all the Sisters used to disappear during that hour. Normally, in a convent, we go to bed early because we get up early in the morning. In some convents Sisters sleep at nine and rise at three in the morning, or we go to bed at ten thirty and get up at five. It is only a small sacrifice when we think of Jesus' sufferings, but somehow we used to become so sleepy during the Holy Hour, and we had to battle against falling asleep. We stayed awake and kept on praying in order to console Jesus for his loneliness and grief when his disciples fell asleep."

Father Yamamoto had never consciously and seriously questioned whether Jesus' death on the cross was God's desire or not. Like many other Christians, he had thought that it was God's plan and was inevitable. Thus, he unconsciously had thought that it didn't make any difference whether the disciples fell asleep or not in terms of how God's providence would have turned out after that. In other words, he never thought that it would influence the outcome of the events of salvation brought by Jesus' death on the cross and his Resurrection. He thought that Jesus' arrest and death were already inevitable by the time of the prayer at Gethsemane. Now Father Yamamoto began to question this.

"Why was it so painful for Jesus to find his disciples asleep in the Garden of Gethsemane? Why did he need to appear to St. Margaret Mary and tell her to pray in order to ease the pain he had from being abandoned by his disciples? If it was all God's plan and inevitable, why did the events cause him so much pain, even centuries afterward? Since we Christians think that Jesus was predestined to be crucified, we just thought that the disciples falling asleep expressed the weakness and helplessness of human nature. Why was it so important for Jesus to have the disciples stay awake and pray with him? If they hadn't fallen asleep, what would have happened? What was Jesus expecting?"

The Roman Governor-General Pilate would let a prisoner go free during the Jews' holy Passover time. When he asked them which condemned prison they wanted set free—Barabbas or Jesus—they called for Barabbas to be set free.

"If the people had said they would forgive Jesus instead of Barabbas...

did all of it depend on the disciples keeping awake and praying with Jesus?"

Unity is considered one of the most important factors for achieving victory or success in projects, sports or in any other activity. Unity between the hearts of people can create something new. It has a strong power to open up the future and can sometimes even cause miracles. Jesus wished his disciples to unite with him, stay awake, and pray with him in the Garden of Gethsemane. If they had felt this desperate desire of Jesus, if they had united with him and kept awake and prayed with him, what could have happened? Could his crucifixion have been avoided by a wave of grace sweeping over the Jewish people, causing them to listen to Pilate's words that Jesus had not committed any evil?

That was something Father Yamamoto couldn't even imagine. Yet did his uneasiness with the possibility come from the fact that he was unconsciously preoccupied with the prejudice that Jesus' crucifixion was God's desire, predestined and necessary for the salvation of humankind?

Jesus prayed three times in the Garden of Gethsemane: "My Father, if it is possible, let this cup pass from me; yet not as I will, but as you will." (Matthew 26:39) When his disciples failed to stay awake, "He said to them, 'Why are you sleeping? Get up and pray that you may not undergo the test.'" (Luke 22:46)

However, they fell asleep all three times. The Christian Churches have interpreted that through this prayer at Gethsemane, Jesus subjugated his own will to that of God, the will that compelled him to go the way of the cross for the redemption of humanity's sins. It has been characterized as a moment of human wavering in Jesus, who nevertheless went on to choose to die on the cross of his own accord.

"Is the true purpose of this prayer different from how it has been interpreted before? Was the prayer at Gethsemane a last ditch effort to save the providence of God that Jesus might live—and establish an earthly Kingdom of God, with himself upon the throne? Have we insulted Jesus all this while, thinking he could have a moment of wavering in the doing of God's will when he was really concerned with the fact that humanity and God would have to continue to suffer in a world of sin?"

When Father Yamamoto came across this question, he thought he somehow found the significance of visiting Paray-le-Monial. Although he still hadn't sorted everything out, he intuitively understood that there was at key here for understanding the true heart of Jesus and solving the contradiction he had been facing.

Jesus' words to Sister Theresa, "Of course, I tried to give the same message" may have perhaps been true. Perhaps the Sacred Heart of Jesus is nobler, more sacrificial, more self-denying than we ever realized—he gave up a crown for a cross because of the faithlessness and lack of support of everyone around him.

So Father Yamamoto began to think as he rode toward Lyon Station in Paris.

The Report on the Revelation of the True Heart of Jesus

A Position More Serious than Luther

March 2008; Vatican

The coronation of the new Pope was over, and the Vatican and the City of Rome were back to normal. The people were gradually getting familiar with the new Pope. The Committee for the Cross Immolation Syndrome began meeting as scheduled. Cardinal Hans Rahner, who was now Pope Pax I, did not attend the meeting. Cardinal Stewart, who was appointed Secretary of the Congregation for the Doctrine of the Faith, took his place and was now in charge of the committee. He also remained the chairman.

After summarizing what had been reported and discussed in the previous meetings, Cardinal Stewart asked Father Yamamoto to report on the new revelation of Sister Theresa. Father Yamamoto stood at the speaker's table, looking tense. The report Father Yamamoto was going to give did not deny that Jesus who died on the cross was the Savior. However, the revelation did state that the cross was not God's initial desire but perhaps was a result of people's faithlessness, thus forcing to the cross the would-be King of Israel, the descendant of King David, in addition to being the Christ. People's lack of faith caused him to sacrifice an earthly throne from which he could establish the Kingdom of God on earth. Instead, he was required to go a sacrificial route of establishing a kingdom in the spiritual realms alone—a glorious spiritual victory that nevertheless left the earth still struggling and sweltering in sin. This was going to be interpreted as denying what Christianity had traditionally believed, although, to Father Yamamoto's mind, it elevated Jesus even higher and glorified him even more. It also affirmed the pervasive sense of tragedy the Catholic Church experienced each Good Friday—that sense that the

Son of Man was killed due to people's faithlessness.

Representatives not only of the Catholic Church but of the entire Christian family were participating in the committee on the Cross Immolation Syndrome. It was clear that what Father Yamamoto spoke of here and how he answered the questions from the participants would greatly influence how the Christian churches would judge the Revelation of the True Heart of Jesus. Naturally, he was more nervous than he had been at the previous meeting.

Father Yamamoto had begun to believe that the Revelation of the True Heart of Jesus was spoken by Jesus himself, and he hoped that others would believe as he did. Some might understand it, as his friend Father Johann Schillebeeckx seemed to. He hoped that many people would accept it, but he was prepared to find many who would reject it.

"Did the religious revolutionary Martin Luther feel this way when he declared, 'Here I stand' at the Imperial Diet at Worms?" he wondered. Would he be branded a heretic—perhaps even excommunicated?

For an instant, he remembered a scene in Germany he had seen while traveling with his friends during summer vacation from his studies in Rome. There was a large and solemn Catholic Church in Worms which seemed to overwhelm everything around it. He remembered that the nearby Protestant church seemed very small and weak in comparison.

Father Yamamoto never thought of himself as being the least bit like Luther. However, what he was about to witness to was the true heart of Jesus which no one had even imagined in the two thousand years since Jesus was born. If that was the case, Father Yamamoto might be in a more serious situation than Luther. He had an urge to flee from the place, but he summoned his courage to go on.

"Jesus wishes to tell all Christians the Revelation of the True Heart. If I can keep a pure heart, wishing to tell people the true heart of Jesus, there should be a way."

Father Yamamoto believed so and began his report, praying for the guidance and protection of God and Jesus.

My Heart Has Been Misunderstood

Father Yamamoto began his report by explaining what Sister Theresa had experienced before Jesus appeared to her again to give her another message. He thought that by reminding them that Sister Theresa had always had a traditional interpretation of the cross prior to this, he could avoid criticism such that she had created the Revelation of the True Heart of Jesus herself, or that she was given to heretical ideas. Father Yamamoto spoke, choosing his words carefully.

"Please remember how Sister Theresa felt when she heard the message of Jesus' revelation, 'I have been misunderstood. Please understand my true heart.' She interpreted Jesus' words based on the traditional Christian view: that Jesus was born with a mission to be crucified and resurrect, but that at that time Jesus lived, no one was able to understand it. Modern Christians don't really understand the true heart of Jesus and have deviated from Jesus' heart and thought little of the value and the significance of salvation through redemption by the cross.

"That is why Jesus gave a revelation to St. Margaret Mary in the 17th century, saying that the Sacred Heart of Jesus, loving humankind with a burning love, should be paid more attention, and that His heart should be revered. Sister Theresa sensed that the Revelation of the True Heart of Jesus is a modern version of the Revelation of the Sacred Heart of Jesus and is a warning to modern secularized Christians. I'm sure you clearly remember how you sympathized with her interpretation.

"She further sought to have a deep interaction in the heart with Jesus, who was crucified for the salvation of humankind. But just as she sought this, she was attacked by nausea in regard to the cross, against her own will.

"It was a very shocking experience and a contradiction for her. She could not understand at all why such an incomprehensive thing was occurring, and she struggled about it. She adores the cross, which was absolutely necessary for the salvation of humankind, and yet the moment she adores it, she feels revulsion too. I'm sure you can understand her struggles to have these feelings, which seem to contradict so much of what she believes and loves.

"But one day, in midst of her struggles, Jesus appeared to her again. She says that through the conversation with Jesus that took place then, she began to feel that she should question the fundamental doctrine of Christianity that the death of Jesus on the cross was God's desire and was inevitable, which was the premise of her interpretation of the revelation to her. Now I will report on why she began to think so."

Thus Father Yamamoto explained that when Sister Theresa said to Jesus that she believed that his death on the cross was God's desire from the very beginning and therefore was his desire, he asked her if she thought believing so meant truly understanding his heart. Father Yamamoto reported that Jesus' response to her was something she had not expected at all, and that she felt quite at a loss. It seemed that her traditional beliefs meant she did not truly understand his heart.

He further introduced the words of the Infant Jesus, "Let's pull out the cross, because it's not necessary," which he spoke when he appeared to her when she was five years old. He had asked her to join him in pulling out the cross from the globe which was like a ball and to roll it together. Father Yamamoto explained that she suddenly remembered these words of Jesus and his sad face. He also mentioned that this led her to think about the traditional view she had never doubted—the fundamental Christian doctrine which she had never consciously thought about on her own.

Lastly, he reported that through her conversation with Jesus, she began to think that Jesus may not have come on earth to die on the cross but rather to build the Kingdom of God on this earth, and thus she came to realize that the very person who had misunderstood Jesus' heart was she herself as well as other Christians who had believed without any doubt that they understood his heart more than anybody else. A dream about Jesus' kingship and his throne made things more vivid to her. Jesus further explained to her in an appearance that her new understanding of his Kingdom and his cross was the essence of The Revelation of the True Heart of Jesus."

Father Yamamoto's report greatly shocked the participants at the meeting. Many of those who had optimistically thought that the series of incidents could be a warning to the Christian church against encroaching materialism (a message they heartily agreed with) now found the revelation different from what they had thought it was. The entire meeting room was now extremely tense.

"How could this be possible? This is Satan's idea. It's complete heresy!" someone cried out.

"It certainly is!"

Some agreed with this, some were silent. All were disturbed and concerned.

"Please be quiet! The report isn't finished yet. Please listen to the end."

Cardinal Stewart tried to calm down the stirring audience. Father Yamamoto continued his report.

"What I have introduced is the essential message of what I have named The Revelation of the True Heart of Jesus. In response to Sister Theresa's question, 'Did you give the same message to St. Margaret Mary?'

Jesus has answered, 'I tried to, but the dogma was a big barrier.'"

There was a stir among the audience again. Father Yamamoto continued in spite of it.

"Jesus knows that Sister Theresa suffered from having been an abandoned child and thus he thinks she is capable of understanding his true heart all the more."

"Does that mean that Jesus was an abandoned child, too?"

"No. I don't think so, because he at least had his mother, Mother Mary, and his foster father, Joseph. We can't be sure just from Jesus' words, but it may mean that he also had a very lonely childhood; perhaps he felt misunderstood even then."

"What are you saying? Jesus spent his childhood in a holy family. That can't be possible. Saying that he had a lonely childhood is a profanation against Mother Mary!"

An Italian Catholic Cardinal cried out and some others agreed with him. A Protestant pastor disagreed with them.

"Well, that is a Catholic way of interpretation. In fact, the Catholic tradition specifically states that Mary and Joseph did not have children other than Jesus by purposely interpreting the word 'brothers' in the Bible as 'cousins'. Since we Protestants in general faithfully interpret the words in the Bible, we believe that Mary and Joseph had children other than Jesus. In other words, we believe that Jesus had brothers and Sisters. Under such circumstances we can imagine that Jesus went through various human emotions; there were perhaps sibling rivalries and feelings of being misunderstood or not receiving enough attention. It is also clear from the Bible that Jesus was criticized behind his back for being an illegitimate child. Surely a child of his sensitivity sensed such social censure."

Cardinal Stewart proposed, "As you have just said, the interpretation of Mary and Jesus' childhood differs between the Catholic Church and other denominations. Other denominations do not revere Mary as much the Catholic Church does. I think that is another discussion. Yet the purpose of the death of Jesus on the cross and its inevitability is accepted in all orthodox Christian churches. I think that we should focus our discussion on that point."

There were many ardent worshippers of Mary among the Catholics, and Cardinal Stewart was anxious that if they went off on that discussion, it would make a difficult problem even more complicated. Some looked dissatisfied, but they agreed to concentrate their energies on discussing Sister Theresa's revelation.

A Heated Discussion

The Cross Immolation Syndrome
as a Sign of Love for Jesus

"Does Father Yamamoto have anything to add?" Cardinal Stewart inquired.

A heated discussion was expected. Father Yamamoto cleared his throat.

"There is one thing I'd like to mention. When we think about immolation of the cross in general, we associate it with people filled with hatred or insanity toward Jesus or toward religion in general. However, in the cases of the Cross Immolation Syndrome that is occurring now, it is quite the contrary. The cross itself is reacted to. This is because, I believe, people are unconsciously reacting to the cross as the instrument used to execute our Lord and Savior. The Syndrome does not deny the messianic nature of Jesus or the value of salvation through the cross. The people involved all accept Jesus as the Messiah, and many are devoted to him. I think that the Revelation of the True Heart of Jesus which was revealed to Sister Theresa is trying to tell us that we should look at Jesus separately from the cross. By doing so, we will be able to see the true heart of Jesus and love him more deeply and with greater devotion. We should not have a hostile view of the Cross Immolation Syndrome, which is related to the Revelation of the True Heart of Jesus. At least, we should refrain from jumping to any conclusion about the faith of its adherents. If we think deeply about the manner of Jesus' death, it is natural that we would feel some sorrow and regret that the Son of God had to be subjected to this. We should not treat those who feel this most intensely according to our prejudice."

"You say 'prejudice', but isn't that saying too much?" asked Cardinal Stewart. Several others also looked upset.

"In the dictionary, 'prejudice' is defined as: 'A perspective or a vision formed about a certain object which is fixed and difficult to change because of the strong effect of the information or knowledge first obtained. Once prejudice is formed, it is difficult to take in any other information which tries to correct it and prejudice tends to positively collect information that affirms it. It is difficult to objectively amend.'

"According to this definition, the view that Jesus' death on the cross was God's plan and was inevitable is indeed a prejudice. Christianity has been convinced of this view and has had a tendency to gather contents that match this view from the scriptures and has either ignored the contents that seemed to deny it or has modified them so that they wouldn't contradict it.

"In order to avoid any misunderstanding, I think we should change the name the Cross Immolation Syndrome to something that reflects the adherents as feeling sadness or pain at seeing a cross."

Cardinal Domenico Cassini of Italy, a worshipper of Mary known for his extremely conservative views, said, "No, I don't think we should change the name. If we change the name and give it a good image, it may appear to give it our stamp of approval. Hearing Father Yamamoto's report, I'm more convinced than ever that the so-called Revelation of the True Heart of Jesus is not from Jesus himself. That is why the name given by Cardinal Rahner, the present Pope Pax I, is completely adequate. 'The Cross Immolation Syndrome' correctly expresses the heretical and anti-Christian nature of the phenomenon that is, I think, caused by spirits that are evil to the highest degree, incomparable to any previous heresy. It undermines Christianity from its very premises and is attempting to alter Christianity into something that is not Christian. The Cross Immolation Syndrome is nothing but a plot by Satan to challenge the entire Christian church. We must stand against it with courage, as true Christians. We should never compromise.

"Please think about it, everyone. Jesus can't possibly deny what Christians have believed for two thousand years. Christians have confessed their faith based on the belief that the cross and Jesus' resurrection were God's plan for salvation and redemption. They have been martyred for this faith. This 'revelation' flies in the face of two thousand years of professed and practiced faith. Can we possibly think that Jesus approves? I trust you all agree with me."

Many applauded him, but many did not. Cardinal Cassini was shocked to see that.

Father Yamamoto was also surprised. Although he couldn't tell what opinion those who refrained from applauding might have, he felt relief that there was not a unanimous outpouring of support for Cardinal Cassini's position.

They had gone way over schedule. They ended the meeting there.

The Greatest Sin and God's Desire

The next day, those who had not applauded in response to Cardinal Cassini's opinion expressed their views. First, a Danish Lutheran pastor spoke.

"My father was a pastor, and I followed in his path. We have had many pastors, generation after generation, in my family. I have worked as a pastor, but embarrassingly, I have had a certain question in my heart for a long time.

"I always told myself, 'I have such a question because I am still immature and do not fully understand the mysteries of the Christian faith. Other Christians do not worry about such a thing, so if my faith and personality develop and if I understand the Holy Bible better, I should be able to have a better understanding.'

"However, the question never resolved itself. The question is: 'If God is love, then how was it possible for God to allow the people of Israel, whom He had loved, chosen, inspired, and guided to kill the one He had promised to them? How could killing the Christ not be a sin?' I thought there must be something wrong with me to wonder so. I thought perhaps I was not suited to be a pastor. However, a friend of mine who was also a Christian had the same question. I could not give him an answer with conviction in my heart. All I could do was to repeat to him what my senior pastors had explained to me. I couldn't help thinking that I was a hypocrite, and I was very conscience-stricken.

"Listening to the report on the Revelation of the True Heart of Jesus, I felt as though a ray of light came into my heart. I thought perhaps my struggle was not wrong or strange. At the same time, I wonder if this is not just a justification of my faithlessness, blindness, and weakness. I am struggling this moment. Yet, unlike in the past, I have some hope. I'm sorry for talking so much about myself."

"Would you tell us in more detail about the doubt you had?" urged Cardinal Stewart as chairperson.

"If God is love, God cannot possibly wish humans to sin. Killing a person is a great sin, but murdering the Christ is an incomparably greater sin. Those who killed Jesus Christ committed the gravest sin, an infinite sin, by killing Jesus, did they not? Yet if Jesus' cross was God's desire, as Christianity has believed, doesn't this mean that God desired the people to kill Jesus? I can't help feeling that this contradicts God's love for His chosen people. Were they chosen, led, educated and guided only so that they could kill the one they had waited for? It does not make sense. The Jews have been persecuted and massacred during the last two thousand years. If Jesus' death on the cross was God's desire, the Jews should be honored as having fulfilled God's desire. They fulfilled their role as the chosen people. Instead, they have been hunted and hounded all over the world.

"I am not saying that is right. Christians never should have persecuted the Jews, because Jesus asked God to forgive the people who were trying to kill him. I am just saying that people had some feeling that killing Jesus was a grave mistake."

There was a stir expressing dissent, but a tall slim Australian Catholic bishop suppressed it and said in a voice loud enough for everyone to hear: "I have something to say that is related to this."

He received a nod from Cardinal Stewart.

"Recently, I was greatly shocked by what a friend in a conservative Catholic monastery told me. He said: 'In order for sinful humanity to be saved, the death of a sinless child of God in our place was absolutely necessary. That is why the death of Jesus on the cross was inevitable and had been planned by God. The person that contributed most to the death of Jesus on the cross was Judas Iscariot. If Judas had not betrayed Jesus, he would not have been arrested and he could not have died and shed his blood on the cross for the salvation of humankind and the redemption of sins. Judas should be revered for making the greatest contribution to the death of Jesus. Yet, how has the Christian church treated him? There has been no one who has been more despised than Judas. In Germany, it is prohibited by law to name a child Judas. What is more, Jesus himself decried Judas's actions, saying that it would be better to have a millstone around one's neck than to have betrayed the Son of Man: woe to him! Why, our congregation has been planning to submit a plea to the Vatican to make Judas a saint in order to justly revere Judas's actions. There is a contradiction here, and I have felt it strongly. I think other Christians feel it too. Am I wrong?"

There was absolute silence.

"We must conclude for now," Cardinal Stewart said. "We will continue our meeting next week."

A courier brought Father Yamamoto a message that he was to call Sister Hostia of the Missionaries of the Consolation of the Sacred Heart of Jesus. He could not meet the eyes of the others who had been in attendance at the meeting as he went in search of a phone he could use in privacy. He hoped Sister Theresa was all right.

When Sister Hostia answered the phone, she barely said a word to him before going off in search of Sister Theresa.

"It's important, that's all I know," she said.

He waited, listening to the whistle of his own hard breathing echoing in the phone. He was happy to hear from Sister Theresa, and frightened at the same time. What new revelation was he going to have to defend before the skeptical committee for the Cross Immolation Syndrome?

"Sister Theresa?" he asked when he heard her soft, humble voice greeting him from the other end of the phone.

"I have had a dream," she said. "A dream so startling—I must tell you about it."

"Please do," he said, his heart in his throat. Then he willed himself to listen.

Sister Theresa had entered the same magnificent cathedral she had dreamed about in relation to Jesus' throne. This time it was full of people. To her shock, they were dressed in clothing suitable to Jesus' time—sandals, full-length robes, and desert head coverings. This was disconcerting. This time the cathedral was decked with more flowers than a person could count—as numerous as the stars in the night sky. Everyone looked happy and excited, and she could see that at the front of the cathedral there were well-dressed dignitaries—priests, scribes, tribal leaders, and even Romans. When the music started, she realized she was at a wedding.

Jesus entered and stood before the altar. He was sumptuously dressed, wearing his crown. When he saw her, he gestured to her to approach the altar.

Sister Theresa swallowed and began to walk forward slowly. Fortunately, no one turned to look at her. Their eyes were fastened on Jesus.

Of course, as a Sister, she was a bride of Christ. She wore a ring to signify that. Every nun became a bride of Christ. Was this the re-enactment of that?

She hesitated to step up to the altar, looking at Jesus for directions. He was smiling lovingly at her, but then he turned to look at someone else who was entering from the side of the altar.

The woman was shining with a spiritual light of great beauty. She did not shine as brightly as Jesus did, and her head was lowered before him, acknowledging him as her Lord. Sister Theresa could not discern her features, but the woman exuded a purity and beauty that was breathtaking. Her spirit seemed to envelop her like a veil, and her face and figure

were indistinct. Her shining white garments were clearly wedding garments, and she came and stood by Jesus' side. He was smiling and proud,
and together they faced the altar, which began to glow with a golden
light so powerful, it was as if the sun had descended directly upon it.

"The Marriage of the Lamb," someone murmured near her, and then
Sister Theresa awoke.

"I cannot think, I am so overwhelmed by it all," she confided to Father
Yamamoto. "What do you think it means?"

"I must think about it some more," said Father Yamamoto. "What was
your feeling during the dream?"

"Intense wonderment—and a sense of what might have been."

They were both silent.

"Let me ruminate on this," said Father Yamamoto. "You think about it
too. If you receive any further insights, please let me know."

"I will. Thank you, Father," she said, her voice small and humble.

The Secret Regarding the Prayer at Gethsemane

An Episode before the Meeting

It was shortly before nine on Tuesday morning, and the meeting was
just about to begin.

Most of the participants had already gathered at the conference room
ten minutes before the meeting started. A Greek-Orthodox priest from
America suddenly strode to the platform at the front of the room and
began to speak into the microphone.

"May I please have your attention? We have special news."

Everyone stopped talking and looked at that priest, wondering what
had happened.

"The Roman Pope Pax I has announced that he is going to recognize
the marriage of priests in the Catholic Church. Let's celebrate this happy
news together!"

There were cries of joy, and everyone stood up all at once. Catholic
priests looked incredulous, but the majority of them looked happy and
applauded.

When the cries of rejoicing died down, the priest at the stage said, "I'm
sorry, everyone. Perhaps I overstepped some boundaries. I only meant it
as a joke. It's April 1st today!"

The atmosphere in the conference room plunged into despair and disappointment.

One clergyman raged, "What a terrible joke! This is too much!"

Then another person said, "I'm not sure about you, but most of the people were applauding, and this conference room was filled with joy for a moment. It's not anything to be angry about. This is a very tense conference. This joke gave us hope and joy even just for a moment."

The priest at the platform said, "I'm sorry, everyone, for deceiving you. I didn't mean to hurt anyone. Please forgive me."

Father Yamamoto, who had also come to the meeting early, pondered. Why this particular joke, now? He felt it had more significance than just a tasteless joke, and indeed, the conversation that followed was eye-opening.

The American priest continued, "You Catholics say that clerics should not be married, giving various official reasons. I have a close friend who is a Catholic priest. He also tries to explain to me why priests don't marry, providing me with various theological reasons. But I know that isn't what he really wants. I have observed him for a long time. When he visits my home, it is sometimes painful observing his lonely facial expression while gazing at my wife and children, although he may not have been aware of it and no doubt tried to hide his feelings. When I saw you rejoice at that moment, I felt that perhaps some of you also yearn for the joy of marriage and family.

"As you know, in Anglican Church and Greek Orthodox Church, only the bishops and high clergy may, by their own will, choose to maintain celibacy. If the Catholic Church had the same system, there would be more people wanting to become priests, and there would naturally be fewer priests who would have secret lovers, abuse children, or be prone toward homosexuality. The marriage of clergy seems to be the trend of the times. I heard that Pope Pax I says that he will positively consider the issue of the marriage of clerics. If there were another Vatican Council, I believe this would be an important issue. Knowing this was the basis of my joke, but I apologize once again for giving anyone false hopes."

"It's time. Shall we begin now?"

Cardinal Stewart had arrived. There was tremendous interest in the topic of the marriage of priests, but the participants settled into their seats, preparing themselves again for further discussion of the Cross Immolation Syndrome.

The Cross and the Problem of the Marriage of Clergymen

The subject would not die, however. An Anglican bishop spoke up to say that he thought the view of the cross in the Revelation of the True Heart of Jesus might contain a positive message regarding the marriage of clergymen.

"Earlier, a Greek Orthodox priest made an April Fool's joke that was, in a sense, relevant to our theme. It seems to me that the celibacy of clergymen and the Revelation of the True Heart of Jesus are deeply related."

"How so?" asked a Methodist priest from Taiwan.

"As you may know, in the early Christian Church, starting with the first disciple Peter, most people were married. (Paul was not.) Although celibacy was respected as a choice, priests were allowed to marry. It was not until the 11th century that celibacy became obligatory."

"What is the theological basis for the celibacy of clergymen?" a Protestant leader asked.

"It has been said that its purpose was to love people universally without limiting one's love to a spouse and family. It was said to be living the lifestyle of heaven in advance, because there is no marriage in heaven. However, I think that the celibacy of Jesus, the teacher, has been the great psychological and emotional basis for maintaining the celibacy of clergymen. Jesus is the model of Christians. He is their ideal and goal. To become a great person means to become like Jesus. It was natural to think that in order to become like Jesus, one had to go the way of celibacy.

"However, what if Jesus did not come to die on the cross but rather to build the Kingdom of God on earth, as the Revelation of the True Heart of Jesus says? Jesus probably would have married and established a family. The King would have a Queen. The Second Adam would have had a Second Eve, in order to truly restore the Garden of Eden, where the first sin took place."

An Italian Catholic clergyman interposed: "Yet even if Jesus hadn't died on the cross, he might not have married."

"Is not marriage a holy estate, given by God?"

"Yes, but some people are called for marriage, and others aren't."

"It seems we are all biologically designed for marriage and family," a Protestant clergyman put in. "Certainly, celibacy is a denial of nature and therefore must be a temporary measure, not a lasting ideal. Perhaps the Revelation of the True Heart of Jesus should be looked on as a joyful sign of the arrival of a new age of understanding: a new era of honor for marriage and family as the original will of God as expressed in the Garden of Eden."

Father Yamamoto felt duty bound to recount Sister Theresa's latest dream. It caused great wonderment and some consternation among the gathered clergymen. However, some were enthusiastic about pursuing the new possibilities if the Revelation of the True Heart of Jesus was true.

"It is strange to say the least that our conversation went in this direction this morning," said Father Yamamoto, "without any prompting from me."

Then, Father Johann Schillebeeckx, a friend of Father Yamamoto, said, "I would like to discuss the fact that the cross clearly *became* God's desire at a certain point, and Jesus went to the cross in obedience to the Father's will. That is indisputable, and it is why Christianity assumes that the cross was God's will all long. Is it possible to think that the cross became God's will at some point during Jesus' lifetime, even if His first or original will was an earthly kingdom and even possibly marriage?"

A Spanish Catholic bishop answered, "When Jesus prayed in the Garden of Gethsemane, his death on the cross was clearly God's desire. From Jesus' prayer in the Garden: 'Take this cup away from me, but not what I will but what you will,' (Mark14:36) it is clear that God wanted him to go that way and Jesus chose God's desire instead of his own and went to the cross. Jesus had a moment of human weakness, yet he chose to do God's will. Otherwise, eternal salvation and redemption from sin through his death and resurrection would have never been brought forth."

"It is possible," murmured an Italian priest, "to interpret those words of Jesus as saying that there *had been* another way possible other than the way of the cross, and that Jesus was hoping that way might still be open."

"There is no remission of sins without the shedding of blood," the Spanish bishop wagged his head in negation.

"Didn't Jesus already have the authority to forgive sins when he was still alive, prior to the shedding of his blood?"

"Ye-es," said the Spanish bishop reluctantly.

The Heart at the Garden of Gethsemane

"Theologian Romano Guardini expresses Jesus death on the cross as the Second fall," some remarked. "The second destruction of the Garden of Eden, an earthly paradise."

As he listened to the discussion, Father Yamamoto remembered the days he had spent at Paray-le-Monial. Since then, he had been thinking much about the prayer at the Garden of Gethsemane. The inspiration he had on the bus had told him that there might have been an important relationship between Jesus' death on the cross and the fact that the disciples fell asleep in the Garden of Gethsemane. He spoke up now.

"As was mentioned, the prayer at Gethsemane has been considered as an influential basis for the claim that Jesus' cross was God's desire. Christianity has interpreted that through his prayer in the Garden of Gethsemane, Jesus understood that the way of the cross was God's desire and he courageously walked the way of the cross, overcoming his human fear of torture and death.

"It has been thought that at that moment, two different wills collided with each other. One was God's will that desired Jesus' death on the cross, and the other was Jesus' will that didn't want to go the way of the cross out of fear or weakness. Jesus even sweat blood on that occasion, so distressed was he. Yet the view that Jesus feared death on the cross out of human weakness has been questioned, both inside and outside the Christian church. After all, Jesus was the Son of God, the Savior. Socrates and other religious martyrs and patriots went to their deaths uncomplainingly, some even praising and thanking God as they went.

"Was there really a battle of wills between God and Jesus? Did Jesus really struggle so much because he wanted to escape from the physical pain of the death on the cross in a moment of human weakness? I wonder."

Father Yamamoto explained that when the disciples fell asleep during the prayer of Gethsemane, Jesus felt abandoned by them. That was why he asked St. Margaret Mary in the Revelation of the Sacred Heart to keep the Holy Hours and stay awake from eleven till midnight on Thursday nights to pray.

"I believe that there is some relationship between the final decision of Jesus to go the way of the cross and the fact that his disciples fell asleep, showing a final faithlessness among the very people closest to Jesus," he told the assembled committee. "Please recall Jesus' parable regarding the master of a vineyard who sent his son so that he would be respected, but his son was killed instead. God Our Father had sent Jesus so that he would be accepted as the Son of God, the Savior. But the people of Israel, in spite of having received prophets and revelations and preparations for thousands of year, did not accept Jesus as the Messiah. They even killed him.

"Perhaps the situation in which the people of Israel disbelieved Jesus was an unexpected, extraordinary situation, completely against the will of God. When even Jesus' own disciples exhibited faithlessness, perhaps God had little choice but to pay the price for the salvation of humankind by sacrificing His only Son, Jesus, on the cross. There was not enough faith on earth to sustain Jesus' mission.

"Therefore, at that point, Jesus' death on the cross became compelling. This doesn't mean that it was so from the very beginning. It may not have been God's desire in the beginning, but the critical situation brought about by the disbelief of the people of Israel and the faithlessness of his own chosen disciples forced Jesus to go the way of the cross. This was not God's original will for him. Perhaps Jesus pinned his last hope on his disciples to stay awake and pray with him, demonstrating their faith in him, to be able to preserve the original will of God. Jesus knew how much grief it would give to God His Father if he went the way of the cross. He knew the tragic fate the people of Israel would have to follow if they killed him, how those who believed in him would have to be martyred and persecuted as he, their leader, was martyred and persecuted. He knew the Kingdom of God on earth would have to be postponed to some future time. He knew humanity would continue to suffer war and deprivation until that time. That was why he searched for a way to avoid the way of the cross until the very last minute.

"However, the disciples did not understand, and they fell asleep three times, although Jesus urged them to stay awake each time.

"Although Jesus lived together with his disciples for three years, teaching and guiding them, in the end they couldn't understand Jesus' heart and couldn't unite with him, and they fell asleep. Would the situation have changed if the disciples had understood the desperate feelings of Jesus and had kept awake and prayed together with him, offering themselves fully to God? Could Jesus have avoided the way of the cross if the disciples hadn't run away when Jesus was arrested? When people are united, an extraordinary power is sometimes created. Perhaps the unity of these representatives with Jesus would have been powerful enough to influence events.

"Sadly, the disciples couldn't unite with Jesus. They betrayed him and said that they didn't know him and fled. So, Jesus had to carry the cross all by himself. If we were in the position of the disciples, we might have done the same. In any case, is it not appropriate to sorrow for their lack of faith and hope to develop our own so that when we are tested in our own small ways, we do not fail the Lord?"

Some were moved by Father Yamamoto's words. He was moved himself; there were tears in his eyes. Every lineament of his body expressed repentance and faith. The meeting adjourned in uneasy silence.

CHAPTER 7
Arrest

The Worst Situation

A Once-in-a-Lifetime-Opportunity

Father Yamamoto felt that he had done the best he could. He believed that there was a possibility for the Revelation of the True Heart of Jesus to be accepted by all Christians. One of the things he thought he needed to do in order to realize that possibility was to see Pope Pax I personally before returning to Japan. The opinion of the Pope would greatly influence the church's viewpoint.

Cardinal Stewart must have given the Pope a detailed report about the meeting, but Father Yamamoto wanted to talk to the Pope in person, both to persuade and to sense what the Pope's thoughts and feelings on the matter were. He had no idea as to how he could arrange this. He could ask Cardinal Stewart, but he wanted to see the Pope alone, without letting anyone know about it, if that was possible.

Time was passing and Father Yamamoto felt distressed. Then something totally unexpected happened. The Pope's secretary gave him a message written on a piece of paper. It said:

"Dear Father Seiichi Yamamoto,

Please come to my office at eight o'clock tonight.

Pope Pax I"

It was extremely unusual for a mere priest to be personally invited to talk to the Pope. Father Yamamoto was surprised and perplexed. Jesus must have been preparing things.

The Pope's initial reaction to the phenomenon was clearly negative, as the name "the Cross Immolation Syndrome" implied. Yet as he had listened to the report regarding Sister Theresa, Father Yamamoto had the distinct impression that the Pope was softening. He didn't know why the Pope had personally invited him to see him, but it was certainly an answer to a prayer.

Father Yamamoto had once taken theology classes from Cardinal Rahner, the present Pope Pax I, while studying in Rome. He had personally visited his office several times to ask him questions, and Cardinal Rahner had welcomed him warmly. However, now that Cardinal Rahner was

Pope, their relationship had changed dramatically. Because of his mission too, Father Yamamoto was tense. Yet when he arrived at the Pope's office, the Pope welcomed him so intimately, it reminded him of his student days.

"Welcome, Father Yamamoto. Thank you for coming. Please sit down and make yourself comfortable."

Pax I offered him a seat. When Father Yamamoto thanked the Pope for the invitation and sat on a sofa, a document on the Pope's desk caught his eyes. It was just for an instant, and he couldn't clearly read the title but he could see the words "statement" and "taking off the cross".

"A Japanese Buddhist representative gave me a Japanese *sado* the other day. Would you like to have some *matcha?*"

"Yes, with pleasure," Father Yamamoto said, pleased to hear the Pope using Japanese. A *sado* was a Japanese tea ceremony set, and *matcha* was the powdered green tea used in tea ceremonies.

"This is not a tea ceremony room, but please imagine that it is."

The Pope personally made Father Yamamoto some *matcha* tea. Then he began to speak.

"This Buddhist visitor told me that the Japanese *sado* originated from an encounter between East and West, which is, I think, very interesting. He said that Rikyu Sen, the person who started *sado* in early modern times, was on close terms with Christians and the influence of the Mass can be found in the tea ceremony. Is this true?"

"I'm not sure if it's true or not, but I have also heard it. It is true that Sennorikyu was on close terms with Christians, and that there are some gestures in tea ceremony similar to those used in giving the Mass," said Father Yamamoto. He demonstrated and some of the similarities between the two, using the tea set.

"I see. Indeed, they are similar," said the Pope with contentment. "The person also told me that there is a relationship between *sado* and Buddhism, and in the spirit of tea ceremony there is a concept of a once-in-a-lifetime opportunity. He explained that when someone invites another person to a tea ceremony, he warmly welcomes the guest as if that is an important once-in-a-lifetime encounter. I was very impressed."

As Father Yamamoto heard these words, he felt that the Pope was trying to tell him that he meant this meeting to be highly significant, and he felt his heart warm.

"By the way, I have a clear reason why I asked you to come. I wanted to hear directly from you what you truly think about the Revelation of the True Heart of Jesus."

The Pope knew well enough from his previous experience as the secretary of the commission that not everything could be reported at the committee meeting, and even if Father Yamamoto was convinced of the Revelation of the True Heart of Jesus, he would have had to speak carefully.

"This is a personal meeting between you and me and, of course, I will not tell anyone what we speak of here. Cardinal Stewart has given me reports on the committee meetings, but there might be some things you could not reveal in public. I would like to hear your honest views."

Father Yamamoto was hesitant as to whether he should completely trust the Pope or not. If the Pope had a negative viewpoint of the Revelation of the True Heart of Jesus, telling him everything might endanger Father Yamamoto's position. They might even make him abandon the priesthood. However, he decided to tell Pope Pax I everything, trusting that God had given him this opportunity. For him, it was now more important that the Revelation of the True Heart of Jesus be accepted than that he guard his own position.

"I will tell you everything I know, feel, and think about it. I was prepared to talk about some of it at the committee meeting if necessary."

Father Yamamoto began to talk about things he hadn't reported at the committee meetings. He told him about his relationship with Sister Theresa and how Jesus revealed that he was with his father, Chuichi, at his surgery, which Sister Theresa could not have known.

He further told him that the words of Janos Gago actually did have a meaning and that in Aramaic they meant 'I did not come to die on the cross.' He explained that these phenomena made Father Yamamoto believe that the Revelation of the True Heart of Jesus came from Jesus himself. He also mentioned that Jesus had told Sister Theresa that he would give her Father Yamamoto as an assistant, but that initially he did not think it had much to do with him.

He also said that Father Minamida told him about the dream his father Chuichi had while he was unconscious after his cancer surgery, in which Jesus appeared and said 'Search for my true heart' and that through these words, he felt that Jesus was not just calling Sister Theresa but also himself. Thus, he began to think of the whole issue as his own.

Then he mentioned his visit to Paray-le-Monial. He explained how he was inspired by the part of the autobiography of St. Margaret Mary where she wrote that Jesus wanted his disciples to stay awake and pray with him in the Garden of Gethsemane. This made him think that Jesus had tried to tell St. Margaret Mary that his death on the cross was not God's desire.

Lastly, he honestly confessed that he now believed that the Revelation of the True Heart of Jesus was indeed from Jesus himself and that the significance of being invited to personally meet the Pope, he thought, was to directly discuss the matter with him.

The Pope listened seriously to Father Yamamoto. There was no doubt he was interested in what Father Yamamoto said, but he did not say anything at all as to what he thought. Father Yamamoto could not tell what the Pope was thinking. The Pope did not seem to be feeling negatively about it all, but he did not seem to be feeling positively either. Nevertheless, being able to meet the Pope personally and tell him everything he knew and thought about the Revelation of the True Heart of Jesus was almost a miracle.

"The rest is up to the Pope himself, to pray and decide." Father Yamamoto desperately wished that the Pope would accept the revelation, but it was beyond what Father Yamamoto could intervene in; it was an area no one could step into. Yet, he somehow felt that there was some hope, and he left the Vatican feeling relieved and refreshed.

Unconscious

Early the next morning, Father Yamamoto heard this unbelievable news on the TV:

"Pope Pax I is unconscious and in serious condition. Was it a heart attack?"

He quickly turned up the volume. It did not seem entirely unlikely, as he knew that the Pope had a weak heart.

"The Vatican doctor responsible for the Pope assumes that the pontiff had an attack and fell sometime between eleven and twelve at night. It is only seventy days since the Pope's coronation. In this emergency situation, conflicting information is emerging, and the Vatican is busy handling many inquiries."

On a different TV channel, a specialist on the Vatican reported in detail how heavy was the Pope's work load and postulated that this work load had triggered the heart attack.

"He seemed so well yesterday," Father Yamamoto mused. Father Yamamoto remembered the encounter he had with the Pope and the Pope's serene smile. He clearly recalled the warmth of the Pope's hand

and arms when the Pope hugged him in farewell.

Come to think of it, there was something that bothered him about their farewell. When Father Yamamoto approached the door after saying good-bye, the Pope called to him.

"Father Yamamoto!"

When he turned back and answered, "Yes?" the Pope seemed hesitant to say something.

Then he had said, "No, it's all right."

What was the brightness in his eyes that seemed to shine with some thoughts that he did not want to put into words?

"I'll see you again."

These were the last words of the Pope.

"The Pope is unconscious and we can make no predictions about his recovery at all. He may not regain consciousness."

As he heard the words of the newscaster, Father Yamamoto thought in anguish: *I should have asked him what he wanted to say.* He regretted not doing so. Yet he had another thing to ponder: *Was the hope I felt after meeting the Pope yesterday merely my imagination?*

Father Yamamoto had begun to believe that he had indeed received a mission from Jesus to spread the Revelation of the True Heart of Jesus worldwide. Pope Pax I was the most important person in fulfilling that mission. But now the Pope was in critical condition. This shocked Father Yamamoto. He felt as if there was an empty hole in his heart as the news cycles repeated the Pope's collapse seemingly endlessly.

The Acting Pope

The Vatican urgently needed to select an acting Pope. They announced that the Head Cardinal, Paolo Toni, the Secretary of the Commission and an Italian, would serve as the acting Pope.

People were extremely sympathetic with Pax I. A rumor was spread that his life was forfeited because he was opposed to "the Cross Immolation Syndrome," a heretical view which was an extreme threat to the Christian church. Many people believed this. Some even said that he should be canonized as a modern martyr if he should die because of this.

Soon a team of doctors announced that Pax I had escaped the danger of death, but because his brain was disabled by the heart attack, the possibility of his regaining consciousness was extremely small. People were very happy that the Pope's life was saved, but they had mixed feelings because the chances were quite high that he would remain in a vegetative state.

The papal appointment is for life. Only if a Pope declares his will to retire is it possible to select a new Pope. However, because the Pope was unconscious, it wasn't possible to confirm his will, and the Vatican kept discussing how to deal with the situation.

Cardinal Toni was a close friend of Pope Pax I from the time they were studying in Rome, and he excelled in both diplomacy and in practical business. He was one of the people Pax I trusted the most. He was known for having moderate views. In this state of emergency, people expected his excellent talents in diplomacy and in practical business to find a way to overcome the difficulties. It was still unknown what view he held about "the Revelation of the True Heart of Jesus."

The Arrest

Someone knocked on the door.

"Who could it be so early in the morning?" Father Yamamoto wondered, and he sleepily opened the door. There were three men standing there. They were policemen.

"I'm Detective Franco Ceroni of the Rome police. Are you Father Yamamoto?"

"Yes, I am. But why are you here?"

"As an important witness of the attempted murder of the Pope, we would like you to come to the police station."

"Attempted murder? Wasn't it a heart attack? What on earth have I done to be involved in this?"

"We would like to ask you more in detail at the police station."

They treated him as if he was a murderer.

"I haven't done anything wrong, so they should be able to understand that if I talk to them," he told himself, and he followed the detective quietly. Because of the blue police car, with its sign "POLIZIA", a crowd of people had gathered to see what was happening. Although he was not handcuffed, two policemen guarded him on both sides. They made Father Yamamoto get into the police car and then headed for the police headquarters. He was feeling more and more anxious.

He found out after he arrived at the headquarters of the police department that Pope Pax I was in critical condition because someone might have attempted to kill him, and Father Yamamoto was an important suspect.

"Wasn't it a heart attack?" Father Yamamoto asked the same question again.

"A new type of poison was found in his body. Father Yamamoto, you were the last person to see Pope Pax I last night. No one saw the Pope after you left him."

"How could I possibly have any motive to kill the Pope?"

"Yes, you do have a motive to kill him."

"What?!"

Father Yamamoto couldn't believe his ears. He was confused, unable to sort all this out. Detective Ceroni took out a piece of paper from his file and placed it in front of Father Yamamoto.

"It is a statement regarding the Cross Immolation Syndrome and the Revelation of the True Heart of Jesus."

The detective began to read part of it out loud.

"Considering the seriousness of the situation, I, Pope Pax I, servant of God, am issuing a statement to all the Catholic bishops and churches on behalf of Jesus regarding the Cross Immolation Syndrome, a series of phenomena which I have decided to call by this name, and the Revelation of the True Heart of Jesus, which Sister Theresa Ueno, a Sister of the Congregation of the Consolation of the Sacred Heart of Jesus in Japan, claims was revealed to her by Jesus himself.

""The Revelation of the True Heart of Jesus" is completely against the precious teachings revealed to the Christian church by Jesus Christ, which have been inherited through the Catholic Church's tradition. In particular, the view that holds that the death of Jesus on the cross was not God's desire, which is the core of the revelation, denies the value of the only, absolute, and ultimate salvation brought to humankind by the death and resurrection of Jesus, and I declare that it is a heretical view.

I add as a part of this statement that whoever believes, spreads, and advocates this heretical revelation should be excommunicated."

Father Yamamoto doubted his ears and tried to confirm it by taking the document into his hands. It was an official statement, written in Latin by Pope Pax I, with his signature and with the papal seal.

"What, then, was that encounter with the Pope all about?" Father Yamamoto wondered. "I can't possibly believe that the Pope showed me such a loving and interested attitude just to interrogate me about my view and then denounce it. If the Pope wrote this statement—no, that can't be possible."

Detective Ceroni interrogated him in an intense tone of voice.

"Do you still insist that you don't have a motive to kill the Pope? You tried to make the Pope accept the heretical view. However, because it was rejected, you tried to murder him, fearing that you would be excommunicated as a heretic. Isn't that true?"

"Detective Ceroni, I didn't know that the Pope had written this until just now. I still can't believe that the Pope has written such a thing."

"Are you trying to say that someone else wrote it?"

"I can't think otherwise."

"Take a good look at this. This is the Pope's signature and the papal seal is properly affixed. Also, we don't find anyone else's fingerprints on it except for the Pope's. Well, everything will be clear as we investigate. We also have a piece of very important information that relates to your motive as well. It is the fact that you were once emotionally involved with the Sister who claims to have received the Revelation of the True Heart of Jesus. You have been deliberately hiding that fact. This is enough to put you under suspicion."

This was something only the Pope knew about. Yet Father Yamamoto could not possibly think that the Pope would have told anyone else. Then who did? Father Yamamoto desperately thought about it, but he couldn't think of anyone.

"Tell us why you met Pax I and what you talked about, in detail."

"It was a personal conversation with the Pope, and I can't tell it to anyone."

"What are you saying! The Cross Immolation Syndrome and the Revelation of the True Heart of Jesus are no longer secret. Don't you understand that you are under suspicion of murder?" The detective made an impatient sound and gesture and took out some newspaper articles from a file. He threw them on the table. In every newspaper, the expressions "Attempted assassination of Pax I," "The Cross Immolation Syndrome," "The Revelation of the True Heart of Jesus," and "Poison" stood out in the headlines.

Father Yamamoto skimmed through the articles and was shocked. Every one of them had contents that couldn't have been written unless the writers knew what Father Yamamoto had told Pax I the previous night. In each of them, Father Yamamoto's name had been raised as a suspect of the attempted assassination. Of course, the content had been skewed, and the articles were written as if the Pope was against the Revelation of the True Heart of Jesus in a similar way as what was written in his statement.

Father Yamamoto felt as though he was having a terrible nightmare. It was very difficult for him to accept that this was actually happening. However, it was true that the Pope was unconscious and in critical condition and could die at any time. Apparently, it was true that there was some sort of poison in the Pope's system. It was also true that he, Father Yamamoto, was suspected of being the murderer and that a statement condemning the Revelation of the True Heart of Jesus as heretical had been issued, apparently by the Pope. All these were facts that could not be denied.

Various thoughts came into his mind. It seemed like forever since he had been awakened by the police on this nightmarish day.

"If I am under suspicion, I should be given a chance to clear my name." So Father Yamamoto determined, and he began to speak, choosing his words carefully.

He told them that he had been personally invited to his office by the Pope, and the Pope had a tea ceremony for him. He told the Pope things regarding the Revelation of the True Heart of Jesus which he had not revealed at the committee meeting. He had also told the Pope about his youthful relationship with Sister Theresa. He then revealed that Pax I had said to him that he regretted having approached the Cross Immolation Syndrome from a negative standpoint initially.

As he spoke about these things, he was more convinced than ever that Pax I couldn't have written a statement condemning the Revelation and its adherents as heretical. Yet, Father Yamamoto did not know how he could prove this—or his own innocence.

A Strange Dream

Father Yamamoto spent lonely, depressing days staring at the gray walls in the prison. Some mornings he woke up and forgot why he was here. Sometimes anxiety and horror would balloon in his heart. Although he hadn't done anything wrong, he felt guilty just being there in the prison. His pain was greater because he had hoped to console Jesus' heart, and now things were coming to a grievous pass.

Father Yamamoto was facing a very severe situation. Attaining his purpose of making all the Christians in the world accept the Revelation of the True Heart of Jesus had seemed difficult enough in the first place. The Pope's statement declaring that the Revelation of the True Heart of Jesus was heretical was fatal to the idea.

The statement had not been declared publicly. Yet the police treated it as a true papal statement. It was clear from the newspaper articles that its content was accepted as authentic by the public, even though no one knew how it had been leaked.

Now he and the Revelation were branded as heretical, and he was imprisoned under suspicion of attempted assassination of the pontiff. The more Father Yamamoto thought about it, the more tragic and unreasonable it all seemed. Yet the thought that he had somehow brought all this about brought him the most suffering. He couldn't even find words to pray. Now he knew what hell was.

Then one night he heard a faint voice echo in his heart. "Your suffering indeed is my suffering."

He couldn't think that Jesus was with him in the prison. It might be more accurate to say that he thought that Jesus couldn't possibly be in such a place. Much less, the pain he was suffering was different from that of Jesus. Yet that thought could not have come out of his own heart.

The voice quietly talked to him in his heart again, as though it knew what was in his mind.

"Have you forgotten that I was also put in prison?"

When Father Yamamoto began to think along those lines, he suddenly remembered each step Jesus took to the cross with a vividness he had never experienced before.

Jesus' disciple Judas had sold him for thirty silver coins. He was arrested, chained up in prison, despised, and beaten. He was then tried in the supreme court, taken to the Roman Governor Pilate and King Herod and was inquired of. Although he was innocent, he was sentenced to death. He was whipped, crowned with a crown of thorns, and forced to carry a heavy cross. He was denounced by the crowd. His disciples denied knowing him and fled. He was stripped naked and humiliated. He was nailed on a cross and pierced in the side with a spear.

Christianity has thought that each of these pains and struggles were not something that just took place two thousand years ago, but they were repeated every time a human being committed a sin. This may be correct, but it emphasized the position of man as a sinner so much that by putting oneself in that position, it created distance from Jesus. This, in the end, led Christians to forget to think about Jesus' heart and feelings and perhaps have made them unable to understand his heart. This may apply to me. Maybe to truly understand Jesus' heart, we need to stand in Jesus' position and experience what Jesus felt and experienced in some way.

Now Father Yamamoto could pray. He said, "Jesus, even if I should be misunderstood and persecuted for the rest of my life, my struggle is nothing compared to yours. Through the little pains and loneliness I am experiencing now, let me feel your loneliness and grief. May this console your loneliness and grief."

After he prayed thus, Father Yamamoto was filled with peace, and he fell asleep.

The next morning he woke up feeling indescribably comfortable, surrounded by something warm. He knew that he'd had a dream, but he didn't remember what it was about or why he was feeling so warm and comfortable. He tried to recollect it with his eyes closed. He then remembered parts of it and then soon he was able to recall the entire dream.

It began with Father Yamamoto guiding a woman in Rome. It seemed to be Sister Theresa. Soon the scene changed, and they were with Pax I, who was sick in his bedroom. Pax I was sitting up on his bed and was speaking to Sister Theresa with a smile, thanking her. There were others in the room, and it was bright and was filled with joy. Then the petal of a red rose fell into the room from the window.

But Pax I was unconscious and Sister Theresa was in a convent in Kyoto, Japan. His dream was impossible. Yet the feeling of being surrounded by something warm lasted for some time, even after he woke up.

Another strange thing happened that afternoon. His friend Father Johann Schillebeeckx came to visit him.

He said, "Seiichi, I went to see Cardinal Stewart before I came here. He told me something interesting. He said he had a dream last night. An Oriental Sister and Pax I were having a peaceful conversation in that dream. He said that even though he has never met her, he somehow thought that it was Sister Theresa. When I told him that I was coming to visit you, he told me to tell you about it. He said, 'It's only a dream, but it may encourage Father Yamamoto.'"

"What?!" Father Yamamoto cried out. "Johann! What a strange thing that is! I had a similar dream early this morning."

Father Yamamoto began to recount his dream to Father Schillebeeckx. Father Schillebeeckx was also very surprised, and they stared at each other. For Cardinal Stewart, it may have only been a dream communicated to encourage Father Yamamoto. However, to them, these two similar dreams were not just coincidental. They were sent to give them hope.

Father Yamamoto felt somewhat liberated from the feeling that he had made an irrecoverable mistake that had led to all this trouble. At the same time, he sensed that Sister Theresa was praying for them.

The Real Statement

Testimony

A new type of poison not still commonly known was used in the attempted assassination of Pax I. Although the lethal dosage was small, its effects were said to be particularly potent for people with weak hearts. Since it worked without symptoms, it was presumed that the suspect used it to make people think that Pax I died of a heart attack.

They still thought that Father Yamamoto had a motive for murdering Pax I, but after investigating thoroughly, they could not find any real evidence against him.

Detective Franco Ceroni had interrogated Father Yamamoto several times, but he could not find any fault with him. He also saw that the priest respected Pax I and seemed sincere and truthful about his last conversation with Pax I. He began to doubt that Father Yamamoto was guilty. The investigation was deadlocked.

Then suddenly some new information came in from an unexpected source. Pope Pax I's brother, Father Martin Rahner, suddenly came to visit the Rome Police Department. He told them that he had some decisive evidence regarding this case. It was a week after the incident.

Father Martin Rahner was three years younger than his brother, and he was working in a church in Freiburg, Germany. He spoke little Italian, so they communicated in English. Father Rahner seemed slightly frightened, and the reason became clear as he spoke.

"My life had been in danger just as my brother's was, and I didn't have the courage to reveal the truth. But, as a priest, I cannot let an innocent person be suspected. I decided that I should speak the truth, risking my life. Father Yamamoto is absolutely innocent. There must be another person who did it."

"How can you be so sure?"

"Because the statement reported in the media is a false one. I have a letter which my brother sent me before the incident, a copy of the real statement, the draft. If you read it, you'll know that Father Yamamoto doesn't have any motive for killing my brother. The draft has corrections in red ink directly made by my brother. If you analyze the handwriting, it should be clear that he wrote them.

"I have never met Father Yamamoto, but I remember my brother saying that he wanted to meet him in person and talk to him. I have also heard him say that he had begun to have favorable thoughts about the Revelation of the True Heart of Jesus. It would be impossible for him to issue a statement that declares it heretical.

"I'm very sorry Father Yamamoto has been kept in prison because of the false statement. This letter was personally written by my brother. It should be sufficient evidence to prove Father Yamamoto's innocence."

Upon saying this, he handed the important materials to the detective. In a letter, Pope Pax I had briefly written in his own handwriting that he felt his life was in danger, and in case he should be killed, he was sending the enclosed copy of the statement and its draft and that all these should be made public in case of emergency. The letter was dated four days before the incident and postal marked three days before it. It was also written that the statement was to be declared at the bishops' conference which had been scheduled on the day after the Pope was poisoned.

On another draft, there were several corrections made in red ink. It was clear that Pax I himself had spent time working on the manuscript. Although it would be confirmed by a handwriting expert, the eye could see that the handwriting resembled that of Pax I when compared to other letters he had written.

"What did Pax I say to you about the Revelation of the True Heart of Jesus?" the detective queried.

"He initially thought that it was dangerous and he thought negatively of it, but when we talked over the phone shortly before the incident, he said, 'Martin, I can't tell you in detail, but the Revelation of the True Heart of Jesus may have come from Jesus himself. If so, it's going to be serious. Please pray so that I can act according to Jesus' wishes.' He pleaded with me to do this."

"If what you said is true, then what Father Yamamoto saw on the desk during his visit was this statement, wasn't it? Does this mean that this original statement was replaced by a false one?"

"Probably, yes."

"Has Pax I shown you such important documents before?"

"No, he never has. This is the first time. He didn't exactly show it to me, but I interpreted that he wanted me to make it public in case something happened to him. He must have really felt his life was in danger. He had been informed that an extremely conservative group wanted to stop him from issuing his statement by all means."

Released

Father Yamamoto was suddenly released from the prison without any advance notice. He had been in prison for two weeks. Detective Ceroni looked sorry for Father Yamamoto, but he didn't explain anything to him because the case was still under investigation.

The investigation was having a rough passage even after Father Yamamoto's release, but the Vatican Office issued a short announcement regarding the assassination attempt of Pope Pax I:

"The attempted assassination of the Pope Pax I is truly a tragic incident. We believe that it was not committed by anyone within the Church. We hope that the Pope recovers, the true assassin will be found, and the truth revealed as soon as possible."

During further investigation, Father Rahner provided Detective Ceroni with some astonishing information.

"To tell you the truth, my brother seemed to have some symptoms of the Cross Immolation Syndrome himself."

"Are you serious? Tell me more."

"My brother called me a week before he sent me the copy of the statement and the letter. According to what he told me then, he always used to kiss the legs of Jesus' image on the entrance wall of his office. But two months ago, he began feeling nausea every time he tried to kiss it. So, he said, he sometimes refrained. He said that perhaps his heart disease could be getting worse, but he also said he couldn't think so because the symptoms were different. He said he was going to monitor the situation for a while."

"I see. Thank you for the important information."

Detective Ceroni thanked Father Rahner and ordered his men to investigate the image of Jesus in the Pope's office. He thought there might be some clue there.

The police also interviewed Cardinal Toni and others relevant to the case. Because it was necessary for the investigation, some of the investigators were informed that there was a real statement and that the Pope himself had symptoms of the Cross Immolation Syndrome.

The Pope Plagued by the Cross Immolation Syndrome

The Struggles of the Vatican

The true assassin of Pax I still had not been found, but some important evidence had turned up. First, there was a hidden microphone installed in the Pope's office. Second, a letter threatening Pax I was found, and thirdly, the poison used was discovered.

According to Father Rahner's testimony, there was an image of Jesus on the cross hanging on the wall near the entrance to Pax I's office. The Pope made it a habit to kiss the legs of Jesus in the image. The poison was found on the surface of the image of Jesus on the cross.

The laboratory investigation made it clear that the poison was very strong, and a very small amount would be lethal for someone with a weak heart. Although the Pope was still unconscious, he was expected to live, and it was considered a miracle.

The police began to think that there was a relationship between this and the testimony given by Father Rahner that Pax I felt nausea upon seeing a cross. The fact that Pax I had refrained from kissing the cross lately due to the influence of the Cross Immolation Syndrome might have saved his life.

However, the existence of the real statement and the information regarding Pope's experience of the Cross Immolation Syndrome quickly became an open secret among the Council of Cardinals. Cardinal Paolo Toni was struggling how to interpret and deal with the real statement. It was only a matter of time before it was leaked to the mass media. So he called an urgent meeting of the Council of Cardinals and revealed the existence of the real statement and its contents and told them not to make it public until the case was truly solved. He also asked the police to keep the existence of the real statement confidential. He was hoping this would give them more time to deal with all the tumultuous events.

The cardinals who attended the meeting were shocked at the contents of the real statement. If its existence was made public, it could shake the foundations of Christianity and put the Christian church into great confusion. What was more, this could afford those individuals and groups who were opposed or hostile toward Christianity a good chance to attack it. They were greatly displeased with the Pope for having tried to issue the statement by himself without conferring with the Council of Cardinals. They didn't believe that the Revelation the True Heart of Jesus came from Jesus himself either.

One of the cardinals remembered the enthusiastic appeal Pax I had made about the critical situation the Catholic Church was facing when he was still a cardinal at the first committee meeting dealing with the Cross Immolation Syndrome.

"What an irony that Pax I, who knew the dangers of the Cross Immolation Syndrome more than anyone else, was invaded by it himself," this cardinal said.

No one knew who had written the false statement, but many of the cardinals thought that the false statement was a more fitting papal statement; so it was all the more convenient for them that Pax I was still unconscious and unable to express his will.

Among the cardinals who were strongly opposed to the Cross Immolation Syndrome as well as the Revelation of the True Heart of Jesus and thought them heretical, some even believed that God had judged the Pope because he was infected by the evil disease and believed the revelation.

But on the other hand, more and more cases of the Cross Immolation Syndrome were being reported throughout the world. In fact, new symptoms were appearing. Some Christians claimed they received revelations directly from Jesus saying, "Take down the cross."

Although they were not instances of the Cross Immolation Syndrome, somehow incidents that involved destruction of the cross by natural disasters such as lightning, earthquakes, tornadoes, and typhoons were occurring with unnerving frequency. This added to the tension surrounding the Vatican at this time.

The Difficult Position of Cardinal Toni

The acting Pope, Head Cardinal Paolo Toni, was faced with a very difficult situation. In general, when a Pope is ill, the acting Pope tries to fulfill the Pope's desires with respect and love. However, in this case, it wasn't so simple.

If he tried to fulfill the desire of Pax I, then he would have to declare that the previous statement announcing that the Revelation of the True Heart of Jesus was heretical was ineffective. He also would have to explain that the previous statement had been forged by someone who had planned the assassination of Pax I.

Then he would have to announce that there was a real statement declaring that the Revelation of the True Heart of Jesus was from Jesus and that Jesus' death on the cross was not inevitable. This also meant that he had to promote what was written in the statement.

Cardinal Toni, of course, knew the contents of the Revelation of the True Heart of Jesus. However, he had been skeptical about it, like most of the cardinals. It would therefore be very difficult for him to stand by the real statement.

Yet, as an old friend of Pax I, he didn't want to do anything to hurt his honor. He didn't agree with the extremely conservative cardinals who insisted that Pax I should be denounced as possessed and heretical. He did wish to protect the Catholic Church from confusion, which he thought was a mission given to him by God. He was determined to do the best he could to find as moderate a way as possible to resolve it all.

He prayed earnestly every day in order to know what to do. He read over the statement by Pax I several times. But Cardinal Toni couldn't understand why the Pope needed to issue it in such a hurry.

"Why couldn't he spend more time making the cardinals understand it and take steps to have it accepted by the entire Catholic Church? Did he want to be a martyr?"

They now knew about the threatening letter sent from "The Association of Christians Protecting Christianity from the Cross Immolation Syndrome," which the police had found in the Pope's room, threatening: "Your life will be in danger if you advocate the Revelation of the True Heart of Jesus."

To Cardinal Toni, Pax I was a self-possessed, calm person and he couldn't possibly think he would dare to do such a rash thing as issue a statement so suddenly. What was more, he couldn't comprehend why the Pope believed that the Revelation of the True Heart of Jesus was truly Jesus' words. He thought that it was not necessary at all to reconsider whether Jesus' death on the cross was God's desire or not.

Pax I had explained in the statement that the revelation came from Jesus himself, and Jesus who revealed it had ordered him to spread it. However, that wasn't convincing enough for Cardinal Toni. He presumed the reason Pax I had to do it in such a way was because the Pope might have thought that there would be an extremely small chance of the other cardinals accepting that the Revelation of the True Heart of Jesus had come from Jesus himself if he went through ordinary procedures.

Since the revealing of the existence of the real statement, Cardinal

Toni had discussed it many times with the other cardinals, but few of them had a positive point of view of the revelation. Rather, the power of the people opposing Pax I and trying to expel him as a heretic was much stronger.

Cardinal Toni thought that the best policy was to hide the true statement and handle the situation peacefully. He wasn't sure people in opposition to the statement and its implications would allow that, though.

He tried to explain to them what a divisive effect the issuing of the real statement would have.

"Many people would claim that it was effective and would try to follow it. Issuing that statement in public is very dangerous and would bring a great confusion within the Christian Church. That should absolutely be avoided," he counseled.

His opponents said, "The Catholic Church is becoming secularized because of just such soft attitudes. We should openly proclaim once again the value of Jesus' death on the cross, the basis of the Christian faith. By this, God will protect the Catholic Church from the evil forces. I know that there are countless Catholics who will stand up. They are looking for strong leadership."

Cardinal Toni honestly didn't know what he should do, so he prayed—and he postponed making a decision.

CHAPTER 8
In Search of the True Heart of Jesus

The Revealed Statement

A Doubt

Father Yamamoto was happy and thankful to be released from prison, but he was wondering how it had happened. He had no idea what was going on at the Vatican and felt a little anxious.

Pope Pax I was still unconscious and unable to function. If his condition didn't improve, a movement calling for his retirement and the selection of a new Pope was likely to come about.

Father Yamamoto was cleared of the charge of the attempted assassination of Pope Pax I, but people looked at him as a believer in the Revelation of the True Heart of Jesus—a heretic. Their attitudes were somewhat cold and unfriendly to him.

Cardinal Stewart had told him and Father Schillebeeckx to stay in Rome and wait for a while. They waited, feeling tense, thinking they might be called by the Congregation for the Doctrine of the Faith and have to face an inquisition, but as the days passed, no direction came. Meanwhile, Father Yamamoto, who didn't know what to do, spent a lot of time with Father Schillebeeckx,

One day Father Yamamoto began to speak to Father Schillebeeckx in a coffee shop where he was certain they would not be overheard. Neither of them knew anything about the subsequent "real statement" that had roiled the cardinals so.

"I can't possibly think that Pax I would issue such a statement," he said.

"But weren't the seal of the Pope and his signature on it?"

"Yes, but ...."

"Maybe you have been deceived after all."

"Do you think that someone who declared that the Revelation of the True Heart of Jesus is heretical would say that he regretted having approached it from a negative standpoint?"

"Then are you saying that the statement was forged? I can understand why you want to say so, and I also wish that was true, but..."

"But don't you think that it's strange? Detective Ceroni who interrogated me said that the reason why I was charged as the assassin was because of that statement. And then, without any explanation, I was suddenly acquitted. This is only a supposition, but if they have found out that the statement was forged, then it makes sense."

"Oh, that can't be true. Are you really serious?"

"I don't know. I just don't know."

The two of them sipped coffee slowly. Father Yamamoto was feeling as if his newfound freedom might be snatched away at any moment.

Leaked Information

Three days after Father Yamamoto's conversation with Father Schillebeeckx, Cardinal Stewart rushed to see Cardinal Toni, who was busy handling clerical matters in the office of the Secretary of State.

"What's the matter, Cardinal Stewart? You seem in a panic."

"Cardinal Toni, we have a serious problem. The existence of the true statement by Pax I has been scooped. The media is in an uproar."

"Who in the world would have done such a thing?"

"We are presently investigating it, but we don't know."

"The only people who knew about it were Pax I's brother, Father Martin Rahner, the Italian police, you and I, and the Council of Cardinals. Father Martin Rahner and the Italian police have promised that they would absolutely not make it public. They, of course, could have broken that promise, but I don't think that is likely."

"Then does that mean it was one of the cardinals?

"I don't know about that either. How was the statement made public?"

"It was made public by someone who considers the Revelation of the True Heart of Jesus heretical and who was against Pax I."

"How do you know that?"

Cardinal Stewart handed a newspaper to Cardinal Toni.

"The news article which was scooped had a headline that said, 'Pope Pax I Invaded by he Cross Immolation Syndrome". The article explained that the Pope had been refraining from kissing the cross, and that the real statement by Pax I was found, which included contents clarifying that he had been possessed by the heretical Cross Immolation Syndrome. It also said that the Vatican was hiding this fact and was trying to defend the Pope and his heretical viewpoint."

"What we have feared has happened. Please call an emergency conference right away," Cardinal Toni ordered. Cardinal Stewart left the room hurriedly.

It was evident to Cardinal Toni that the information had been leaked by the opposing group. They must have presumed that leaking the information would force Cardinal Toni to declare the Revelation of the True Heart of Jesus heretical. Naturally, it would bring a conviction against Pax I. Thus, Cardinal Toni thought that the only measure he could take was to declare what Pope Pax I had said in his statement about the Revelation of the True Heart of Jesus, declare it effective, and follow it. That was what he had to do as acting Pope, in Pax I's place. It would not be easy, because he himself did not believe it.

Yet he could not possibly believe that the measure the opposing group took was the godly way. He expected great confusion to follow what he proposed to do, but it seemed to him that there was no other way. Besides, he thought that the other cardinals would agree with him.

However, when an emergency conference was called for, he was shocked. Most of the cardinals were opposed to his proposal.

"There is no other way left to solve this situation other than to convict as heretical the Revelation of the True Heart of Jesus," the cardinals urged.

For Cardinal Toni, who did not believe in it, it was not such a problem to declare that the Revelation of the True Heart of Jesus was heretical. Yet he had thought for certain someone would insist, "The true statement has force as the Pope's statement, even if Pax I is unconscious, and we should follow it." Cardinal Toni had feared most that, in such a case, the Catholic Church would be split.

He also worried that if the Catholic Church publicly declared something was heretical, it would recall the dark past of the Inquisition in the Middle Ages and this might tarnish the image of the Catholic Church. What was more, he owed loyalty to Pax I. Indeed, he was torn.

In spite of him, a decision was made by the majority to make the true statement by Pax I public and to declare the Revelation of the True Heart of Jesus heretical and announce that Pax I had been invaded by the Cross Immolation Syndrome. Against his will, Cardinal Toni had to accept it.

That night, he wrote a statement to be issued to all the lay members and those in holy orders in the Catholic Church throughout the world. Ironically, its content was almost the same as the false statement forged by the group that had claimed it acted to protect the Christian Church from the Cross Immolation Syndrome—the same group that had tried to assassinate Pax I. This is what Cardinal Toni wrote:

Statement Regarding "the Revelation of the True Heart of Jesus" and the Cross Immolation Syndrome by the Council of Cardinals

I, Paolo Toni, the Acting Pope and the Chief Cardinal, representing the Council of Cardinals, solemnly make an announcement in order to fulfill my mission of leading the Catholic Church in the correct direction, following the decision made by the conference of the Council of Cardinals.

My statement is in regard to the Cross Immolation Syndrome and the so-called Revelation of the True Heart of Jesus. The last statement by the Pope was forged, and a true statement exists separately. I will first read my statement.

Our Catholic Church is facing a critical situation such as we have never faced before in history. I truly hope that Catholics, both lay Catholics and those in holy orders, will be totally united and overcome this crisis in order to protect the precious faith we have inherited.

The crisis we are facing involves the worldwide phenomenon of the Cross Immolation Syndrome, which makes people detest the cross and seek to immolate it, coupled with the movement of believing that the heretical message of the so-called Revelation of the True Heart of Jesus came from Jesus himself. What we grieve the most is that Pope Pax I, whom we have elected, has been affected by the Cross Immolation Syndrome.

The Revelation of the True Heart of Jesus claims that Jesus' death on the cross was not God's desire and that Jesus came on this earth in order to live and establish the Kingdom of God. This denies the fundamental Christian doctrine. If we leave this assertion unanswered, the value and significance of Jesus' cross are denied, and Christianity is no longer Christianity.

Like many others, I have loved and respected Pax I. Everyone acknowledges his life of devotion to the Catholic Church, his pre-eminent knowledge in theology, and his noble personality. Because of all these factors, the Council of Cardinals elected him Pope.

Sadly, the battle between God and Satan is beyond our imagination. The very person who realized the danger of the Cross Immolation Syndrome sooner than anyone else and who called the meeting for counteracting the Cross Immolation Syndrome and made efforts to protect the Catholic Church from its threat has been invaded by it and related heresies.

Pax I has been refraining from kissing the adored cross, a custom kept by Pax I himself and dear to the Catholic tradition everywhere. This is described in the statement by Pax I. Symbolized in this behavior, Pax I has clearly been affected by the Cross Immolation Syndrome and has deviated from the Christian faith.

It is painful and sad that someone has attempted to assassinate Pax I and that the Pope is still unconscious. However, had Pax I remained well, it is clear that he would have used his authority as the Pope of the entire Catholic Church to accept the heretical so-called Revelation of the True Heart of Jesus, as is written in that statement.

The Council of Cardinals solemnly declares in order to protect the Catholic Church from the Cross Immolation Syndrome that the so-called Revelation of True Heart of Jesus is heretical, and therefore the statement issued by Pax I is not effective as an official papal statement. Furthermore, we declare that whoever believes that the so-called Revelation of the True Heart of Jesus comes from Jesus himself and spreads it is a heretic.

In this critical time, I deeply wish all to recognize again the fundamental Christian doctrine that claims that Jesus' cross and his resurrection are the only, absolute, ultimate salvation and to enjoin all to be united and to make efforts to protect the Catholic Church from Satan's plot.

The Acting Pope

The Head Cardinal

Paolo Toni

Cardinal Toni could not believe that he was doing anything wrong toward Jesus and the Catholic Church in writing the statement. It was a short night, but he peacefully fell asleep.

A Historical Day

It was two o'clock in the afternoon the next day, and the shocking statement declaring that the Revelation of the True Heart of Jesus was heretical and that Pax I had been invaded by the Cross Immolation Syn-drome was to be announced worldwide. The statement written by Car-dinal Toni was already placed on the speech table. St. Peter's Square was filled with people, and the sky above it was cloudless and cleardinals strongly opposed to the Revelation of the True Heart of Je-sus were looking forward to the presentation of the statement. Not only

Catholics, but the whole world was watching with breathless anticipation via television broadcast. Cardinal Toni looked a little tired, but he had a refreshed expression on his face as though something had been cleared in his mind. Soon he stood at the speech table and began to speak in Italian in a very clear tone of voice.

"Today, I am issuing a very important statement. It has to do with the real statement by Pope Pax I, whom we love and respect. As you may know, someone almost poisoned Pax I to death. Fortunately, his life has been saved, but he is still unconscious and the doctors' opinion is that there is little chance for him to recover. In spite of valiant police efforts, no suspect has been arrested.

In this emergency situation, I, Paolo Toni, the Head Cardinal and the Acting Pope, make this important announcement to you in order to guide the Catholic Church in the proper direction. This announcement is based on discussion at the Council of Cardinals, but ultimately, I am taking the responsibility as the Head Cardinal in making this presentation.

First of all, the last statement by Pax I issued as a papal statement has been proved by the police investigation to have been forged by those who plotted the Pope's assassination, and the real statement has been discovered."

There was a stir among the crowd at St. Peter's Square. The group of Cardinals that knew the content of the statement that was to be presented today caused a commotion.

"What is going on?"

Sensing that something unexpected was happening regarding Cardinal Toni's presentation, some Cardinals thought that they should stop him. However, no one could do anything since the presentation was taking place facing a large crowd gathered in St. Peter's Square and telecast as well as disseminated via Internet throughout the whole world. In spite of the Cardinals, Cardinal Toni continued to speak.

"Secondly, Pax I's actual view of the Cross Immolation Syndrome and the Revelation of the True Heart of Jesus was completely the opposite of what was written in the false statement."

There was another big stir among the crowd, but Cardinal Toni continued to speak.

"The third announcement, which is the most important, is that the content of the true statement by Pax I is still effective even in the present situation in which Pax I is unconscious, and all Catholics, both lay people and those in holy orders, must accept its content with respect."

"What is going on? That's not what he was supposed to say!"

Cardinals who were strongly opposed to the Revelation of the True Heart of Jesus were furious. The many TV cameras, however, meant that they even had to refrain from showing such feelings with their facial expressions. What was more, the speech was being sent out over the Internet as well.

"This statement by Pax I includes an important message which will greatly influence the Catholic Church, all the Christian Churches, all the other religions, and the future of the entire world. It is at the same time, a question posed to each and every person who is listening to this message. Please open up your hearts and listen to the statement by Pax I which I will now read to you with a prayerful heart."

After this introductory remark, Cardinal Toni began to read the true statement of Pope Pax I. As he read aloud, an incident that had happened at dawn that morning was strongly in Cardinal Toni's mind.

Why Do You Persecute Me?

After he finished writing the statement late the night before, Cardinal Toni went to bed only to be awakened by a dream at dawn.

In the dream, he heard a voice saying, "Paolo Toni, why do you persecute me?"

"Who are you?"

"I am Jesus, whom you are about to persecute."

"Lord, that is not possible. I love you and I have offered all my life to you and to your church. How could I ever possibly persecute you?"

"Indeed, you have loved me, devoted your entire life for me, and have done your best for the development of the Catholic Church. But have you ever thought about my true feelings?" asked Jesus.

Cardinal Toni found himself attacked by anxiety. The peace he had felt the night before disappeared.

"It's only a dream," he tried to convince himself to calm his heart. But the more he tried to do so, the more Jesus' words spoken in the dream echoed in his heart.

"Paolo Toni, why do you persecute me?"

These words were similar to the words Jesus spoke to the greatest evangelist of early Christianity, Paul, when Jesus appeared to him after the Resurrection. Paul, called Saul, was a Pharisee, and he was an earnest believer who had been convinced that Jesus was a false prophet who profaned God. He was persecuting Christians, catching and even trying to kill them.

Saul then was hit by lightning and fell off his horse while on his way to Damascus to persecute Christians.

"Saul, Saul, why do you persecute me?"

Hearing a voice speaking to him, Saul questioned, "Lord, who are you?"

"I am Jesus, whom you are persecuting," the voice answered.

This is the famous incident that converted Saul, who had been greatly feared as a persecutor of Christians, to become the most devoted Christian evangelist, St. Paul.

Cardinal Toni felt more and more anxious, but he intended to carry out what had been agreed by the Council of Cardinals and what he himself believed was best for the Catholic Church.

"That must have been Satan's temptation."

He tried to shake off his anxiety by believing so. Then, at that very moment, his heart began to beat abnormally fast. It was so unbearably painful that Cardinal Toni fell on the floor. He had never been ill and had confidence in his health. He had never suffered such a symptom before. He suffered and struggled so much that he thought he might die. Then he clearly heard a voice echo again in his heart.

"Paolo Toni, why do you persecute me?"

Cardinal Toni could no longer doubt that the voice was that of Jesus. He shuddered at what he was about to do.

What a mistake I was about to make!

He thought that is was much better to die at that moment than to persecute Jesus. If issuing the false statement as the true one constituted persecution of his Lord, he would not do it. He felt more thankful to Jesus for stopping him from committing a dreadful crime at the very last minute than he felt fear of dying. In the midst of intense pain, pain so bad he thought he would die from it, he plucked all his willpower to do what could be done at the very last minute. He crawled on the floor to his desk and managed to take up a pen and a piece of paper. He wrote:

Cardinal Toni's Will

I declare that the Revelation of the True Heart of Jesus comes from Jesus Christ himself.

When he finished writing it and whispered, "I entrust my spirit to you, Lord," strangely, that dreadful, deathly pain in his heart quietly disappeared.

At that very moment, he discerned everything clearly. The statement was scheduled to be issued in the afternoon of that day but there was only one road to go. It was to follow Jesus.

In Order to Console the Pain of Jesus

Cardinal Toni began to read out loud the real statement by Pax I:

Statement Regarding the Revelation of the True Heart of Jesus

I, Pope Pax I, as a servant of God and a shepherd responsible for all the children of the Catholic Church, hereby issue an important statement for all those in holy orders and for all lay believers.

It is regarding the phenomenon of the Immolation the Cross, the symbol of Christianity, which is occurring all over the world, and the Revelation of the True Heart of Jesus, which is closely related to the phenomenon, in which Jesus himself is said to have appeared and revealed to Sister Theresa Kokoro Ueno, a Sister of the Missionary of the Consolation of the Sacred Heart of Jesus in Japan.

It was I that named the phenomena occurring in various parts of the world that seemed to deny the cross "the Cross Immolation Syndrome" and it was I who suggested to the late Pope to call a committee to counteract it. I was the chairman of the committee until I became the Pope.

Initially, I looked askance at the Revelation of the True Heart of Jesus. I convened the committee from that standpoint. However, as I thought over all the reports, and after communion with God and Jesus through prayer, I gradually came to understand that the name the Cross Immolation Syndrome was far from what those phenomena truly meant and was quite inadequate.

Now I confess to you that I believe that the Revelation of the True Heart of Jesus is a revelation given by Jesus himself. Jesus' death on the cross was never God's desire. God sent Jesus to this world because he wanted him to live and establish the Kingdom of God on this earth.

However, for the last two thousand years Christians have believed that Jesus came on this earth to die on the cross and that the cross was God's desire as well as Jesus'. By this, they have misunderstood Jesus' feelings and have crucified him an infinite number of times.

When I found this out, I do not know how much I wailed. As a Christian who loves Jesus, how could I not wail, discovering that Jesus has been living a lonely life with such a sorrowful, misunderstood heart?

By the mystical guidance of God, I was given the responsibility of the

Roman Pope, to be the head of the Catholic Church, the successor of Peter. If there is something I must do in the mission as Pope, it cannot be other than fulfilling Jesus' desire.

Yet I am sure many of you will wonder in your mind why I am issuing this statement without consulting other cardinals.

I also thought many times, over and over again, that I should not announce this statement without their knowledge and consent. When I asked Jesus what I should do in my prayer, however, I heard Jesus clearly saying, 'Announce it right away without consulting anyone so that the glory of God will be revealed.' I went beyond my own thoughts and ideas, and followed Jesus' words, entrusting myself to Jesus' desire.

Jesus desperately wants each and every Christian to understand his sorrowful and lonely, misunderstood heart. If so, what can be a more important mission for a Pope to accomplish than to convey this message?

One may label me a heretic Pope who has been invaded by the Cross Immolation Syndrome. I also initially thought that it was all heretical. But once I discerned by the guidance of the Holy Spirit that Jesus' cross was not God's desire, seeing the cross made me sad. My heart ached and I started to feel nausea. When I tried to kiss the cross as I used to, I no longer could do it because I started to feel sorrow and pain in my heart.

This experience made me understand that it was not because they detested Jesus that Sister Theresa and others, whom I had not thought well of, felt nausea seeing a cross or painted out the crosses in paintings or tried to destroy them by fire.

I finally came to understand that because they had more sensitive hearts than others, they were able to somehow sense that Jesus did not wish to be crucified and Jesus expressed to them his feelings about how he did not desire the cross.

This statement does not impose upon anyone to believe it. I know well that faith should not be imposed on anyone. This is a confession of my faith. I am only fulfilling the responsibility I think I should fulfill as Pope, as the successor of Peter. I believe I should accomplish this even at the risk of my life, and that by doing so, I may be able to console the struggles, sorrow, and loneliness of Jesus.

Yet what Jesus is aiming for in the Revelation of the True Heart of Jesus is not his consolation alone. It leads to a universal ideal, peace in the world, which all of humankind is searching for. The Revelation of the True Heart of Jesus does not deny that Jesus is the Messiah. However, the understanding that Jesus did not come on earth to be crucified may open a path for a dialogue with Judaism, which traditionally understood that the Messiah came to establish a Kingdom of God on this earth.

A path for reconciliation not only with Judaism but also with Islam, Buddhism, Hinduism and many other religions could also open. The cross, the beautiful symbol for Christians, has been raised at times for the purpose of war and conquest. For those peoples, the cross is an object of fear, symbolizing the massacres committed by the Crusaders, the persecution of the Jews by Christians, and the destruction of local religions and cultures by missionaries. If Christians relinquish the cross, it could pave the way toward a new era of understanding.

It is extremely sorrowful for Jesus to see the divisions within the Christian church. The Second Vatican Council (1962-1965) called the Protestant Church a separated brother and opened up an epoch-making way for unity within the Christian church.

We must humbly admit that the Catholic Church, like other Christian churches, is imperfect and has made many mistakes in the past, and that it presently has many problems. Jesus is showing us the way we should walk through the Revelation of the True Heart of Jesus. It is a way that leads to unity within the Christian church, a way to reconciliation among different religions, and a way to realize peace on earth.

I believe that a Christian who truly loves Jesus would certainly understand what I am talking about. There may be a great confusion created within the Catholic Church. We may need to reexamine the original doctrine which was based on the preconceived view that Jesus came in order to be crucified, and we also need to reflect on the symbol of the cross, which is a symbol of tragedy and injustice. Rather, we should reflect on Jesus' love and forgiveness for the Jews and the Romans, even while he was on the cross. Jesus' ability to love even his enemies is the true emblem of Christianity. Were we able to emulate this love, I think many tragedies could have been avoided.

Now is the time for us to express our faith in Jesus and our love for him. Indeed, this is the time. My heart is trembling with a hope for the arrival of a new era. The true heart of Jesus has been revealed. This means that we are living at a time as significant as two thousand years ago when Jesus was on earth.

God and Jesus wish to establish Kingdom of God on earth filled with love, peace, joy, and happiness, and we must fulfill this wish and realize it.

I pray that God may bless you, your families, and your countries. Servant of God's servant,

Pope Pax I.

As Cardinal Toni read aloud this statement, he felt touched by the desperate feeling of Pax I in trying to issue his statement at the risk of his life. He knew that those in opposition were going to say, "Cardinal Toni has been invaded by the Cross Immolation Syndrome."

However, that no longer mattered to him.

"This feeling can perhaps be understood only by those who have truly experienced feeling Jesus' heart."

Cardinal Toni thanked God that he had been able to finish reading the statement issued by Pax I, and he honestly did not care what might happen to him personally now.

A Sign of Change

Among the Crowd

Both Father Yamamoto and Father Schillebeeckx were among the crowd in St. Peter's Square, listening to the announcement made by Cardinal Toni. When Cardinal Toni finished reading the true statement written by Pax I, Father Yamamoto said in his heart to the unconscious Pope Pax I: "Thank you for writing this. You are truly a great Pope. You witnessed to Jesus' true heart at the risk of your life. This is so precious. I am grateful to you."

He also thanked Cardinal Toni in his heart, because he could easily imagine how difficult it had been to make the decision to read the statement. Although it was actually happening in front of him, Father Yamamoto was almost afraid to believe that it was true. He felt that Father Schillebeeckx, standing next to him, was also feeling the same way.

Father Yamamoto was absorbed in his emotions for a while. Many people were very shocked at the message of the statement, but most people did not clearly understand what was happening. Yet the statement read aloud by Cardinal Toni had a power that moved people's hearts.

Soon he remembered that when he was just about to say good-bye to Pax I, the Pope seemed to want to say something to him. It occurred to Father Yamamoto that the pontiff probably had wanted to tell him that he also believed the Revelation of the True Heart of Jesus. He tried to think why Pope Pax I hesitated to tell him on that occasion. Father Yamamoto speculated that the Pope might have thought that if he confessed it to Father Yamamoto, it might put him in danger, and he may have wanted to protect his life. When he thought thus, Father Yamamoto's love for Pax I deepened even more.

He remembered his classes and the times he visited his office when the Pope was still a cardinal. He was loved by many students because he was so modest and he would kindly answer any questions the students had. He lived a simple and strict life. Father Yamamoto had once visited his room and found it strange because there was no bed. He later heard from another priest that the future Pope slept on a sheet of thin cloth on the floor. And now, with Cardinal Toni's reading of the true statement clearing Father Yamamoto of all suspicion in the poisoning of the Pope, Father Yamamoto felt he owed his life doubly to the Pope.

"How splendid it would be if Pax I were still in good health, if he could continue spreading the Revelation of the True Heart."

That was no longer possible. It was true the situation was now more joyful than before, but when he thought of the Pope's condition, Father Yamamoto couldn't help feeling sad.

How does God see the present condition of Pax I? Is it a sorrowful situation for God just as it is for me?

When he began to question it, he thought he could feel the sorrowful heart of God seeing the present condition of Pax I. He wondered if this was something like the sorrow God felt upon seeing His only begotten son crucified and unable to build the kingdom on earth.

Father Yamamoto wiped his suddenly flowing tears, hiding his face from Father Schillebeeckx.

The Pilgrims

The announcement by Cardinal Toni as acting Pope caused reverberations around the world. Rumors and criticisms spread. Some said that the false statement was actually the real statement and that this statement was forged by Cardinal Toni, a victim of the Cross Immolation Syndrome. Other Christian Churches reproached the Catholic Church for having done such an absurd thing. Cardinal Toni was astonished by the intensity of the reproaches and criticisms, although he knew they were to be expected.

However, some unexpected reactions also occurred. Some accepted the statement uncritically. They devoted themselves to Jesus in their prayers. Some received answers in their prayers that Jesus did not come to be crucified. Others were touched in their hearts to know that Pax I had tried to declare the statement at the risk of his own life, and they began to pray for his recovery. Some came all the way to St. Peter's Square to pray. What surprised Cardinal Toni most was that among the pilgrims were people wearing the attires of other religions. The numbers grew larger day by day.

The media began to take an interest. Some of these pilgrims were interviewed in a news program on TV and they made it clear why they were in Vatican City.

"We did not come here as tourists. We came to pray for Pax I's recovery."

Cardinal Toni's heart burned with joy when he saw people of different religions giving similar answers. The interviews continued, and many people watching were moved to see that the Pope's courage and outreach had drawn people of other religions to come pray for him.

Not so the cardinals. The cardinal stormed into Cardinal Toni's office and asked him to explain why he had read a different statement without their consent. Cardinal Toni called an emergency meeting to give an explanation.

He showed them the statement he had written before going to sleep that night. One of the cardinals read it out loud. They nodded, as its content was what they had agreed upon.

They were confused: "But why didn't you read this statement?"

"I had an astonishing dream," he said, and he told them about the dream in which Jesus said to him, "Paolo Toni, why do you persecute me?" He recounted how he still had not been able to believe the Revelation of the True Heart of Jesus, even after the dream. The moment he thought that it was Satan's temptation, though, he felt a violent pang in his heart and fell. Then he heard a voice saying again, "Paolo Toni, why do you persecute me?" He could not help believing that it came from Jesus.

"That's absurd!" was the collective reaction of the cardinals.

"Why is it absurd? Jesus is still living and working now, just as actively as he was in St. Paul's time. Why can he not speak to us now? I admit, I still couldn't believe it even after my dream, but when I heard the voice again and was struggling unto death, I discerned that Pax I was right. I was convinced that we were guided by the Holy Spirit to select him as the Pope. We must fulfill his wish."

Some of the cardinals were moved by what Cardinal Toni said.

Cardinal Stewart said, "Come to think of it, there was an expression, 'Our times are as significant as when Jesus was alive.' I don't think that

Cardinal Toni is lying. Perhaps we have no other option but to believe Cardinal Toni and unite."

A number of cardinals agreed with him. The cardinals who were opposed remained silent. Cardinal Toni began to speak again,

"It may also take me some time to accept that Jesus' cross was not God's desire. It may be the same with you. That's natural, since it goes against what we have always thought. However when I started to reflect on it calmly, I began to realize that some results of research in modern theology support the messages of the Revelation of the True Heart of Jesus.

The Revelation of the True Heart of Jesus does not deny the messianic mission of Jesus, nor does it deny the value of salvation through the cross and the resurrection. However, it focuses more on the possibilities inherent in Jesus living on this earth to establish the Kingdom of God as a temporal as well as a spiritual reality—'Thy will be done on earth as it is in heaven.'

We may, in fact, look at the Revelation of the True Heart of Jesus as something Jesus gave to us to in order to open a new era based on previous Christian history rather than as something in conflict with the previous traditional interpretation. The Revelation of the True Heart of Jesus was given because of Christian history up to now. Its time is now.

The point is that we need the humility to honestly reexamine Christian doctrine and have the hearts to try to understand Jesus' true heart and that he was born to build the Kingdom of God on earth, as a literal as well as a spiritual King of Kings."

The cardinals were relieved and reassured by what Cardinal Toni said.

One of them remarked, "Most of the issues Martin Luther put forth leading to the Reformation, which caused him to be excommunicated at the time, were accepted by the Catholic Church 450 years later at the Second Vatican Council. When we consider that, there might have been a way to avoid the split at that time, the fracturing of the Christian church, had people had open minds. An open attitude towards Judaism and other religions, promulgated at the Second Vatican Council, also seemed very new at the time. If we consider this, perhaps the present issues may not seem so extraordinary."

The Council of Cardinals as a whole began to feel some hope for the future, even though some cardinals continued to murmur among themselves. As a whole, the Council of Cardinals was beginning to trust and follow Cardinal Toni.

They were encouraged by the many letters they received from around the world stating that people were hoping and praying for Pax I's recovery. In spite of the statement, or perhaps because of it, an unprecedented amount of love was being poured out toward the Roman pontiff.

In Order that the Glory of God Will Be Revealed?

Cardinal Toni was making effort to realize Pax I's wish. People's view of Father Yamamoto and Father Schillebeeckx became considerably more favorable.

The opposing group was claiming that Pax I's statement was not effective because Cardinal Toni issued it in opposition to the decision made by the Council of Cardinals. Some conservative thinkers campaigned in various ways to spread the news that this was indeed Satan's intrusion into the church.

They did not oppose it simply because they wanted to defend themselves or because of any evil intentions. Rather, it stemmed from their love for Jesus, in whom they believed. They were convinced they were doing the right thing out of loyalty to him. That was why the problem was complicated, and resolving the situation peacefully didn't appear to be easy or even likely.

Cardinal Toni consulted with Cardinal Stewart and some other cardinals and decided to gather prominent theologians and have them study the Revelation of the True Heart of Jesus from a theological standpoint and see if it harmonized on any points with traditional Christian doctrine. When news of these efforts spread beyond the Catholic Church, various other Christian denominations offered to cooperate and began to send theological theses which could contribute to the work.

However, the opposing group still resisted and insisted as follows:

"If the Revelation of the True Heart of Jesus is from Jesus himself, there should be some miracles or some supernatural signs attached to it, just as Jesus worked miracles and as the saints have miracles attributed to them. No miracle has been performed related to the Revelation of the True Heart of Jesus. Pax I is still unconscious; he is nearly dead. He must have fallen into such a miserable state because he acted against God's will."

The condition of Pax I in the severity of his illness, rendered unconscious and unable to do anything, indeed did seem to be preventing the Church from being united and moving forward as one body.

As was becoming his habit, Father Yamamoto consulted Father Schillebeeckx.

"Johann, how do you think we should deal with this confusion?"

"It's probably difficult to resolve it right away. Seiichi, do you have any ideas?"

"No, I don't have any ideas, but I can't help feeling that there is something that hasn't been done yet. I feel that it's not the end yet."

"Well, Cardinal Toni has already accepted the Revelation of the True Heart of Jesus, and the entire church is moving in the direction of acceptance. You've done well. I think it's better for us to withdraw at this point."

"I'm not thinking at all that I have done well. If I ever think so, I lose the value of everything I have done up until now. But somehow, I feel that I shouldn't go back to Japan as things stand. I feel there is more so that, as Pope Pax I said, 'the glory of God will be revealed.'"

"Well, your intuition has astonished me before. I would be willing to trust it now. Of course, the person who tried to murder Pax I still hasn't been arrested, and we still don't know anything about who else was behind the attempt. Pax I is still unconscious. If you are saying that things are not settled or cleared up, you're right. But hasn't God's glory already appeared enough because the Revelation of True Heart has already been accepted by Church leaders and people of various religions are visiting the Vatican to pray for Pax I's recovery? I've thought so."

"I initially thought so, too, but I'm beginning to feel that was not the end of it."

"What do you mean?"

"Jesus speaks these words in the Bible in a scene where he performs a miracle to heal a sick person. As you may know, Jewish society at that time thought that illness was a result of sins of the individual or of ancestors. Jesus avoided such discussion and said from a completely different viewpoint that the man was ill 'in order for God's glory to appear' and then he healed him.

"Those who are opposed to the Revelation of the True Heart of Jesus believe that Pax I believed in a heresy and that he tried to spread it using his authority as Pope and that he was almost poisoned to death and fell into a miserable unconscious state as punishment. Don't you think their way of thinking is similar to that of the Jews living at the time of Jesus?"

"Yes, I can see that."

"I think that everything will fall into its place if Pax I recovers from his illness in a way that is somehow relevant to the Revelation of the True Heart of Jesus."

"Seiichi, are you saying that some miracle needs to occur?"

"Yes, but I feel that we need to do something for that miracle to occur."

"Are you saying that you are going to make a miracle happen?"

"When Jesus performed miracles, he would often say, 'Your faith has saved you.' I think that it means that the miraculous healings performed by Jesus required faith in the human beings present. I think we need to unite the faith of everyone that believes that the Revelation of the True Heart of Jesus comes from Jesus. Then I believe a miracle will happen."

"What do we need to do?"

"At the moment, I don't know. But as we start moving forward with faith, we should be able to discover it. Jesus will show us what to do. I think Pope Pax I is a precious, loving disciple of Jesus who has truly inherited the heart of the Lord. I cannot possibly think that Jesus intends to leave him unconscious and on death's doorstep."

A few days after this conversation, Father Schillebeeckx called Father Yamamoto.

"Seiichi, something flashed in my mind. Let's meet at our usual coffee house in two hours."

"All right. Something has flashed into my mind too."

They met at the coffee house, ordered espresso, and immediately began to talk.

"Let's say it at the same time."

"All right. One, two, three!"

"The dream!!"

"It's the dream!"

"We were feeling the same thing!" they said and laughed. What flashed in their minds was the dream that both Father Yamamoto and Cardinal Stewart had, in which Sister Theresa was at Pax I's bedside.

Father Schillebeeckx said excitedly, "You and Cardinal Stewart had a similar dream. There must be meaning in two people having the same dream. Pax I recovered consciousness in both dreams. Sister Theresa was in Pax I's bedroom in both dreams. You said that Pax I was expressing gratitude to Sister Theresa in your dream. You also mentioned a red rose. I don't know what the red rose means, but isn't this dream telling us that Pax I is going to be miraculously healed by Sister Theresa?"

"I was thinking exactly the same thing," said Father Yamamoto. "But Sister Theresa is in a convent in Kyoto and not in Rome."

"Then we have to bring her to Rome. That might be quite difficult. You cannot bring a Sister from a convent in Japan unless there is an order from a bishop or for some extremely special reason."

"It may be impossible."

"But you could ask her if Jesus has given her any new revelation since then, just in case. You could tell her what we are thinking now and also about the two dreams."

"You're right. I'll call her in Japan tomorrow."

Sister Theresa's Prayers

International Phone Call

It was eleven o'clock in the morning in Rome. In summer time, the difference between Rome and Japan was seven hours. It was six o'clock in the afternoon in Kyoto, and it was dinner time in the convent, which was a good time to call.

Father Yamamoto first contacted Bishop Hayata and explained to him the situation and asked for permission to talk to Sister Theresa over the phone. The Bishop seemed to trust Father Yamamoto. He said that he would contact Sister Hostia, the director of the convent. For Bishop Hayata, Father Yamamoto was a pride of the Kyoto Parish.

When Cardinal Toni read the true statement issued by Pope Pax I, Bishop Hayata was watching him on TV with other priests and Sisters in the bishop house. They were amazed to hear Sister Theresa's name mentioned. Although Father Yamamoto's name was not mentioned, everyone could imagine that he had made a great contribution to the announcement of the statement.

Sister Theresa herself knew little about all the developments in Rome. She spent her time in dedication and prayer, as always. She was therefore perplexed to find Sister Hostia, who transferred the call to her, kindly proffering the phone.

"This is Sister Theresa," she said into the phone after taking it from Sister Hostia.

Father Yamamoto heard the clear voice of Sister Theresa over the phone. She sounded just the same as the last time they had spoken.

"I had to call you because there is something I must consult you about. You must be surprised, aren't you, to hear my voice?"

"Yes, but I'm also relieved. You sound well. Bishop Hayata told me that you were having a very difficult time, and I was worried. I'm sure that you worked very hard supporting Cardinal Toni in making that historical announcement. I'm deeply grateful to you."

"I thank you. You have supported and encouraged me greatly through your prayers," said Father Yamamoto. He briefly recounted to her his visit to Paray-le-Monial and what had happened since leaving Japan for Rome. Sister Theresa didn't say much, but he could feel from the atmosphere of the conversation that she knew about his arrest and had been worried about it. Her concern made him happy. Soon he explained to her why he was calling her, coming around to the main issue.

He told her that there was still something left to do in order to realize Jesus' wishes and that he felt he should not return to Japan yet. He further explained that he thought that there must be some important meaning in the words of Jesus 'for God's glory to appear' and what he and Father Schillebeeckx had talked about regarding the dreams. Finally, he told her the conclusion they reached. He could feel that she was seriously listening to him over the telephone.

Through the conversation, he found out that she had been praying for the Pope's recovery both in solitude and with all the Sisters in her convent, and that she too had a feeling that something more had to be done.

Regarding the dream Father Yamamoto and Cardinal Stewart had in which she herself went to the Vatican to heal Pax I, her response was very restrained and hesitant. He was not sure if it was because of her modest personality or because she did not agree with their interpretation. She said that she had received no further revelation from Jesus.

"If you sense something in your prayers, please tell Sister Hostia and contact us. We are facing an urgent situation. Although we do not have your consent yet, we're going to ask Cardinal Stewart to convince Cardinal Toni to invite you to the Vatican. I think it's difficult, but not impossible."

"Why should I meet the Pope? I am not important enough," she whispered. "But I will pray that Jesus' wishes will be realized."

Her name had appeared in the real statement by Pax I read by Cardinal Toni and the attitudes of Sister Hostia and the other Sisters had started to change toward her after that, which was uncomfortable for her. She did not like to be noticed in any way. She couldn't dream of doing something extraordinary in public, such as visiting the Pope in hopes of effecting a healing. She thought that her mission had been fulfilled at the point when Father Yamamoto accepted the Revelation of the True

Heart of Jesus. Yet, she had not had peace in her heart for a moment since Cardinal Toni had made that historical announcement.

Since the Pope had fallen ill and into unconsciousness, she had been earnestly praying for his recovery. She was ready to do anything in order for him to be healed. However, going to Rome herself to heal Pope Pax I was something she had never dreamed of.

However, since Father Yamamoto had called her, she started thinking that if she could console Jesus' heart by doing so, she should be determined to do it, no matter how difficult it might be.

The Possibility of an Invitation

The next morning, Father Yamamoto and Father Schillebeeckx visited Cardinal Stewart in Cardinal Toni's room in the Congregation for the Doctrine of the Faith.

"Cardinal Stewart, there is something I would like to talk to you about," Father Schillebeeckx began. "Do you remember the dream you had when Father Yamamoto was in prison?"

"Of course, I do. It was a very impressive dream."

"We asked you for your time today because we wanted to talk with you about it."

"Really? What do you want to say about it?" asked Cardinal Stewart curiously.

"When I told Father Yamamoto in prison about the dream as you told me to do, he said that he had the same dream."

"What? A similar dream? Do you mean the Pope met Sister Theresa in your dream, too?"

"Yes," said Father Yamamoto, and he told him about the dream. Then he told him that they interpreted that the two dreams were significant to the Revelation of the True Heart of Jesus and that perhaps Jesus wished to help Pax I recover from unconsciousness. The cardinal listened earnestly.

"Well, then, what was it that you wanted to ask me about?"

"We would like you to ask Cardinal Toni to officially invite Sister Theresa to come to Rome. We would like to challenge the possibility of a miraculous recovery based on her presence."

"I think I can do that, but I wonder if Sister Theresa has received a new revelation from Jesus and has been given some direction from him on how she could heal the Pope. If so, I think it would be easy for me to talk to Cardinal Toni about it and for him to accept it."

"Well, on that point, I have already asked Sister Theresa about it, but she was doubtful. She said that she has not received any new revelations."

"I see. Then in that case, I may not be able to convince Cardinal Toni to invite Sister Theresa to Rome based solely upon your interpretation of two dreams."

"We think so, too. Could she be officially invited just for being the Sister who received the Revelation of the True Heart of Jesus?"

"I don't think it's impossible. That could be meaningful. Perhaps that would be of less of a burden on Sister Theresa, too. Would that be all right?"

"Yes, of course!"

They both thanked Cardinal Stewart for the way he handled the situation and left his room.

"If Sister Theresa could come to Rome, something might develop," they assured one another, trying to think positively.

Reunion in Rome

Sister Theresa left Osaka Kasai International Airport for Rome in order to meet Pope Pax I. She found it strange to be on board an airplane. She knew in her mind that it was a wonderful grace to be able to pray for the Pope's recovery from nearby, but she still could not feel how that was actually going to happen.

The letter inviting her to come to Rome, which she received through Sister Hostia, was an official letter from the acting Pope, Cardinal Toni. A Japanese translation was attached to it. The letter said:

Letter of Invitation

"I believe that if Sister Theresa Ueno, who received the Revelation of the True Heart of Jesus, comes to visit Pope Pax I, who has been unconscious ever since he tried to tell the world about the revelation, risking his life, it would avail much. Therefore I, the acting Pope, Paolo Toni, invite you to come to Vatican to pray for Pope Pax I at his bedside."

It was also added in the invitation letter that it was to be a two-week visit and that the Vatican would provide the round-trip air travel fare and the accommodations. Although Sister Theresa thought it would be presumptuous of her to accept it, in obedience, she did. She did, however, ask the Vatican through Bishop Hayata not to make this invitation public. It would not be true to say she was not anxious, but she could only entrust everything to Jesus.

She was to stay in the Headquarters of the Convent of the Congregation of the Consolation of the Sacred Heart of Jesus during her stay in Rome. The only Japanese Sister who belonged to the congregation in Rome was going to meet her at the airport to help guide her, because Sister Theresa couldn't speak Italian or English.

On board the airplane, Sister Theresa was recollecting how her life so far had been guided by Jesus and the incidents that had led her to go to Rome. She thought that the number of atrocious crimes, massacres, wars, and sorrowful incidents in which many people lost their lives because of poverty and illness was increasing every day. Humankind, unable to realize a peaceful happy world full of joy in spite of much searching and effort, was still suffering and groaning in agony.

She reflected on how many people trembled with anxiety and hopelessness about the future, thinking that happiness and peace were mere illusions. Although Sister Theresa also had no idea of what kind of future awaited the world, when she thought of her own mysterious path, guided by Jesus every step of the way, she felt hope that someday a happy world would surely be realized.

She heard from Bishop Hayata that Father Yamamoto had gone through many hardships in order to testify to Jesus' heart. It was very painful to her to hear that he was imprisoned because she thought it was because of her. She had prayed fervently for his protection. She became excited thinking about Father Yamamoto's devoted life, Father Schillebeeckx's friendship and support, and above all, Pope Pax I's love for Jesus at the risk of his life.

There are people who understand Jesus' true heart and who are trying to love Jesus, she thought. She hoped that the sorrowful, broken heart of Jesus, misunderstood for the last two thousand years, would gradually be healed by the accumulated efforts of such people.

Father Yamamoto was waiting for Sister Theresa to arrive at the Leonardo da Vinci Airport in Rome. The Japanese Sister of the Congregation of the Missionaries of the Consolation of the Sacred Heart of Jesus had fallen ill, and Cardinal Stewart had called Father Yamamoto, along with Father Schillebeeckx, to go to the airport to guide Sister Theresa in Rome.

Various memories flashed back in Father Yamamoto's mind: the time he left Kokoro Ueno behind and ran to Shijou-Kawaramachi in Kyoto crying out, "God!" The long period of time he struggled because of his actions, even though he was saved by choosing to become a priest. He remembered their reunion and their encounter with the Revelation of the True Heart of Jesus, the scene of the cancer surgery of his father, Chuichi, which he heard about from Father Minamida, and the dream his father had, as well as the time when he visited Paray-le-Monial. He also recollected the report he made at the counter-acting committee meeting and the discussions they had at the meeting. He thought of his arrest and subsequent release from prison.

"Who had ever imagined that such a day would come when we would meet again?" he marveled. "If we trace all of it back, it all may have begun when Sister Theresa was still Kokoro Ueno and was spending her lonely childhood in a children's home. The heartfelt encounter between Jesus and Sister Theresa there laid the foundation that later moved my heart and in the end influenced Pope Pax I and the Catholic Church and led to the announcement to the entire world of the arrival of a new era."

Thinking thus, Father Yamamoto really felt that the invisible heart-to-heart interaction between Jesus and Sister Theresa was precious and irreplaceable.

"How does Jesus feel meeting this Sister coming from Japan?" Father Yamamoto thought that he was somehow feeling the deep affection Jesus had for her.

He had to wait for a while, but soon Sister Theresa in her habit with a suitcase appeared, looking somewhat anxious. She seemed surprised to find Father Yamamoto waving his hand at her, but she waved back at him happily.

Father Yamamoto suddenly remembered Sister Theresa slightly waving her hand at him with a forced smile when he looked back to see her after leaving her alone in front of a movie theater.

"Is that her?"

Father Yamamoto came to himself at Father Schillebeeckx's question, and when they were near to her, he explained to Sister Theresa why he was there to meet her. Then he introduced Father Schillebeeckx to her. The three of them headed for the headquarters of the Congregation of the Missionary of the Consolation of the Sacred Heart of Jesus. Father Yamamoto translated what the Sister of the convent said to Sister Theresa, and they arranged their schedules. The next day they had an appointment to meet Cardinal Toni at four in the afternoon. They decided to go sightseeing in Rome before the four o'clock meeting.

The next day, they met at the convent where Sister Theresa was staying and went to see the Coliseum and Foro Romano. Sister Theresa seemed to find everything she saw unusual and fascinating.

When they were having lunch, Sister Theresa suddenly asked in a serious tone of voice, "Father Yamamoto, will you please tell me about the dream again?"

The two men looked at each other. They had thought that Sister Theresa did not want to talk about it.

"We thought you didn't want to talk about it."

"Well, it's still the same now, but I'm concerned about it."

"I see," said Father Yamamoto and told her again about the dream he had and about the dream Cardinal Stewart had. "Then a red rose petal appeared, and..."

"What? A red rose?! You never mentioned that over the phone!"

"Well, I may not have mentioned it when we talked over the phone. It seemed such a small detail. Is there some significance to a red rose?"

"No, there isn't. It's probably all in my mind."

The two of them understood that she was sensing something, because she suddenly looked extremely serious, as though something was on her mind, but she would speak of it no more.

Petals of Tears

The three of them headed for the Vatican after lunch. They left a little early so that Sister Theresa could visit St. Peter's Cathedral before their appointment with Cardinal Toni. There were many people of different religious backgrounds from various countries among the Christians in St. Peter's Square, praying for Pax I's recovery, which was a strange and beautiful sight.

After visiting St. Peter's Basilica, they met Cardinal Stewart in front of it and headed for the Pope's office where, as acting Pope, Cardinal Toni was receiving important guests from all over the world. It was the room where Father Yamamoto had met Pax I. The cross placed near the entrance door that had been used for the attempted assassination had been removed. Father Yamamoto remembered the day Pope Pax I had invited him to see him.

Cardinal Toni warmly welcomed the three people introduced to him by Cardinal Stewart, and gave them a big smile.

"You have done a great job believing in the Revelation of the True Heart of Jesus and telling the world about it in spite of many difficulties.

I thank you from the bottom of my heart on behalf of Pope Pax I."

He thanked Sister Theresa and the two priests. He particularly expressed his deep gratitude to Sister Theresa for coming all the way from Japan to visit Pax I at his bedside.

"I thank you, Cardinal Toni, for proclaiming to the world the effectiveness of the true statement in spite of great difficulties you had to go through," returned Sister Theresa.

Cardinal Toni looked pleased at her words. Father Yamamoto and Father Schillebeeckx nodded many times and expressed that they also felt the same way about Cardinal Toni. Although they each had different positions in the church, they felt that they were united with each other for having walked the same path in search of the true heart of Jesus. They had a peaceful interlude talking with one another.

"Now I will take you to where the Pope is," said Cardinal Toni, and all of them went to the room where Pax I was deep in sleep.

Pax I was surrounded by medical equipment and many tubes were inserted into his thin body. He slept like a living corpse. It was painful and sad for three of them to think that this was the outcome of his noble action of being willing to sacrifice his life in order to console the broken heart of Jesus. A Vatican doctor and a Sister tended the stricken Pope.

Sister Theresa approached the bedside. She closed her eyes and began to pray quietly. The others naturally joined her. Even after the others opened their eyes, Sister Theresa was still praying. People around her could feel how deeply she loved and respected Pax I from the way she prayed.

After a while, her intense facial expression relented into a peaceful smile. Soon a trickle of tears started from her eyes. They did not appear to be tears of sorrow. Her face was impassive; nor did she sob. They were quiet peaceful tears as Sister Theresa communed deeply in heart with God.

When she finally finished praying, her eyes had an infinite clarity and were full of purity. She had seemed to lack confidence before, but she now seemed like a different person. She was beautiful and full of spirit.

"I was very anxious before I came here. I started to feel this anxiety the moment I received an international phone call from Father Yamamoto. Father Yamamoto said, 'I feel we still need to do something.' Later, he told me that Cardinal Stewart and Father Yamamoto had similar dreams on the same day. When I heard this, I agreed with Father Yamamoto that there was something more to be done.

"I began to think that I perhaps should do something so that Pax I would recover consciousness. I was struggling, thinking that I was too small a person to do such an extraordinary thing. All I could think of was to pray. I asked Jesus what I should do, but there was no answer.

"Then, while I was having lunch with Father Yamamoto and Father Schillebeeckx earlier this afternoon, they told me that there was a red rose petal in the dream. When I heard this, I began to have hope, thinking that there might be a way. Now in my prayers, I have communicated with Jesus and that hope has turned into conviction."

She removed a pendant from around her neck.

"I used to wear a cross until I received the Revelation of the True Heart of Jesus. Now I wear this pendant. This pendant is very special and precious for me. It is a symbol of the encounter I had with Jesus."

She opened the pendant and showed it to everyone. Everyone approached and looked at the small pendant.

"A red rose!"

It was Father Schillebeeckx who cried out. There was a small red rose petal encased inside the pendant.

"It was on the day that I understood for the first time that Jesus' death on the cross was not God's desire. I was crying, thinking about the pained heart and feelings of Jesus who had been misunderstood for two thousand years without anyone knowing the truth. This feeling exposed the arrogance in my heart that had made me believe that I knew Jesus. I was so sorry that I could not raise my head. Then Jesus shed tears, and his tears touched my face. I haven't told Father Yamamoto about it, or anyone else, but the tears that touched my forehead dropped on a rose in a nearby vase."

"Is this the rose?"

"Yes, it is. This is the rose petal touched by Jesus' tears."

Everyone looked curiously at the small red rose petal in the pendant. It took their breath away. Quite some time must have passed since it fell, but it still had a vivid fresh color as though fallen from the flower only moments ago.

"I thought this must be the red rose petal that appeared in Father Yamamoto's dream when he told me about it at lunch today, but I was not sure until I prayed about it more. Now after my prayer, I am convinced that it was."

"Did Jesus say so in your prayer?"

"Not exactly, but I feel it in my heart. I can now see a light of hope.

May I ask you to do something?"

"Of course," answered Cardinal Toni.

"'I would like to have a special time to offer a special prayer for Pope Pax I's recovery together with the people down in St. Peter's Square. Could you announce 'Please all be united in heart and pray'?"

She had such a firm attitude that Father Yamamoto flustered hurriedly to translate her words. Cardinal Toni ordered Cardinal Stewart to do exactly as she said. Soon the message Sister Theresa asked for was announced repeatedly by Cardinal Stewart in Italian, English, French, Spanish, and in German so as to reach the diverse group of people gathered in St. Peter's Square.

The people at the square were puzzled by the abrupt announcement but thought that it must be important and began to pray whole-heartedly. Some prayed in tears. Some did not understand what the announcement meant, but they saw what the others around them were doing and followed them.

When Cardinal Stewart returned to the room, Sister Theresa said to the people gathered there, "Everyone, please touch the Pope's body and pray for his recovery. Please believe that Jesus truly loves the Pope and wishes him to recover."

Sister Theresa took out the rose petal from her pendant and placed it on Pax I's lips. Then she put her hand on the Pope's forehead and began to prayer in a barely audible voice. Father Yamamoto interpreted the prayer.

"My beloved Jesus, we know how much you love Pax I, for he has understood your true feelings and has tried to sacrifice his life in order to console your sorrowful and lonely heart.

"That is why we know that just as you did not desire Jesus' death, you do not wish Pax I to die. My beloved Jesus, just as the Pope believed your words, we also believe your words. Now is the time for God's glory to appear. Please wake the Pope from his unconsciousness."

After that she continued to pray in silence. After a while, her face began to flush. Everyone could see that she was in a deep spiritual communion with Jesus and was having a dialogue with him. All the people watched her closely and were moved in their hearts by the scene. They thought that this must be like the experience the saints had of intimate encounters with God known as the "beatific vision," which they had read about in the lives of the saints.

Soon, they all began to smell a very fragrant aroma, although they did not know where it came from. It smelled like a sweet rose.

Just then, the rose petal placed on Pax I's lip moved slightly. The indicators on the medical equipment that had hardly been moving gradually began to move. Then Pax I's eyelids trembled, and soon his eyes opened.

Everyone was speechless. The most surprised among them was the Pope's own doctor, whose prognosis was that the Pope would never regain consciousness.

"Cardinal Stewart, please tell the people at the Square, 'Your prayers have been heard, and Pope Pax I is recovering. God's glory has appeared.' And thank them."

Hearing these words from Sister Theresa, Cardinal Stewart dashed out. Cardinal Stewart, usually so calm, was full of excitement. His voice, making the announcement, soon resounded in St. Peter's Square. After a moment's silence, applause and shouts of joy arose. Whether Catholic or Protestant, Christian, Jewish or Muslim, the people all hugged each other and praised God, celebrating this joyful miracle. Soon the bells, usually only used when a new Pope is selected, were ringing. The sun was setting, but people would not leave the Square. Their faces were shining under the setting sun.

Was this a miracle? If it was a miracle, Father Yamamoto thought, it was a miracle caused by a heart-to-heart interaction with Jesus. The moment Sister Theresa understood Jesus' heart, Jesus' heart was touched and he shed tears. His infinite love was condensed in the teardrop that fell upon the rose. While Jesus' love could not be seen with physical eyes, it worked with wondrous power to forgive and cleanse people's sins, to get rid of conflict and hatred, and it remains a power that heals loneliness, sorrow, division, pain, and illness. It is a power that, once tapped with faith and love, brings joy, peace, and happiness.

Epilogue

Pax I recovered rapidly. Within a week, he was taking light meals as well as liquid food. Soon he was able to walk by himself. He vacated his sickroom and returned to his own room.

The first day he returned to his room, Sister Angella Rotti, who was taking care of his meals, approached him as he searched for a book, and she suddenly burst into tears in front of him.

"What's the matter, Sister Angella? Has anything happened?" asked Pax I.

"Holy Father, please forgive me! I did it!"

Pax I could not understand what she was talking about.

"I put the poison on the foot of Jesus' image on the cross!"

Pax I was speechless and incredulous for a moment. Sister Angella, sobbing, began to tell her story haltingly.

"Cardinal Cassini is my uncle on my mother's side, and he is my god-father. He said, 'The Pope has been affected by a heretical view called the Cross Immolation Syndrome. This is the only way to protect the Catholic Church.' I could not believe it at first, but Cardinal Cassini told me the same thing over and over again, and as I saw you refrain from kissing the cross, which you used to do, and as I saw you getting sick seeing the cross, I began to think that what Cardinal Cassini was saying might perhaps be true. Oh, what a dreadful sin I have committed! What shall I do?"

She burst into tears again. She kept crying for some time.

Pax I approached her and laid his hand on her shoulder and said in a calm voice, "Sister Angella, do not worry. No one will judge you. I will not blame you, either. You do not have to cry any more."

She looked up at the Pope for a moment, looking as though she could not believe it. His eyes were smiling warmly. When she understood that those words came from his heart, she began to wail even louder.

Pax I let her cry for a while, then he said, "Will you serve me just as before? As if nothing happened?"

"Are these the words of someone I tried to murder?" she wondered in her mind.

"Do you like to serve me?" the Pope asked in a quiet voice.

"Of course, yes. I hadn't even thought about such a thing, continuing to serve you. I would be happy to serve you. Thank you very much."

"Please tell Cardinal Cassini how I feel, and please cook that delicious special spaghetti you cook for me again," said the Pope, smiling, and he returned to his bedroom. Even after he was gone, Sister Angella stood there, rooted to the spot, overwhelmed with sorrow and gratitude from her radical encounter with someone capable of forgiving and loving his enemies.

A few days later, Detective Ceroni called Father Yamamoto and said that he wanted to see him. Father Yamamoto did not know why the detective would want to see him, but he decided to go.

The first thing the detective said was, "Please forgive me for what I have done to you. Also, I am sorry that I still cannot arrest the true culprit. Actually, I retired the other day and I am no longer a detective. So I am here today to see you not as a detective, but as a private citizen, Franco Ceroni."

Father Yamamoto thought that Detective Ceroni looked young for having reached retirement age.

"Please do not worry," he reassured him. "You only did what you had to do. You've worked hard for a long time, and it is good that you are retiring. Was there anything else you wanted to talk to me about?"

"Father Yamamoto, may I ask you a favor?"

"Of course. I will be happy to help you in any way I can."

"I would like to meet the Holy Father in person. Would you be the mediator? I think you have that kind of influence."

"For what purpose do you want to see the Pope?"

"It is something personal."

"I see. The Pope has not completely recovered yet, and I am not sure if it's possible, but I certainly will ask him."

Father Yamamoto called Cardinal Stewart on the spot and explained the situation to him. Cardinal Stewart called him back and told him to come two hours from then, with Mr. Ceroni. Father Yamamoto was surprised at the quick response.

Mr. Ceroni already suspected who was the real culprit in the attempted assassination of Pax I, but he had not told anyone. He wanted to see the Pope and confirm something. He thought that it would not be too late to tell his superior at the police department about it after that. However, now that he was retired and no longer in charge of the case, it was very difficult to see the Pope as a mere citizen. That was why he had decided to ask Father Yamamoto for help.

It is a great honor to meet the Pope in person as a citizen. Yet no desire for fame or honor made him want to see the Pope. He wanted to know how the Pope would react to the naming of the culprit who had attempted to assassinate him.

Furthermore, he was beginning to have great interest in the Revelation of the True Heart of Jesus, which had been creating a sensation ever since Father Yamamoto's interrogation. One of the reasons why he wanted to personally meet the Pope was because he wanted to see the Pope, a person who was willing to risk his life for his faith.

"Holy Father, I came here to inform you of a very important thing," he began his conversation with the Pope.

"You're talking about Cardinal Domenico Cassini and Sister Angella Rotti, aren't you?"

"How do you know?" asked the astonished former detective.

"Would you believe me, if I said that Jesus told me?"

The Pope smiled a mischievous smile. Mr. Ceroni thought that could be possible, given the series of incidents that had occurred. But he hesitated to answer.

"Mr. Ceroni, you have retired, and you no longer have obligations as a detective. I ask you as a citizen. Would you leave everything you know about the attempted assassination case with me?"

"Aren't you going to file a complaint against them?"

"I have no intention of accusing or judging them. I do not wish them to be arrested or punished."

"You are not going to level charges? They tried to kill you!"

"Mr. Ceroni, what is the purpose of judgment or punishment?"

Mr. Ceroni stuttered, "I think they make criminals compensate for their crimes and hopefully bring them to remorse so that they never commit the same crime again."

"I think so, too. Of course, there could be different cases depending on the kind of crime committed and the individual circumstances of the suspects. However, as far as this incident is concerned, I think that this is the best conclusion. I did not die, and I have no intention of accusing them. I think that Jesus would do the same. I trust that they will compensate for the crime they have committed by serving others and will never commit such a crime again. Do you think that you could do more by arresting them, accusing them and judging them guilty and punishing them? I think that they have already become aware of the sins they have committed by seeing me given life again by Jesus."

"But…" Mr. Ceroni began to say something, but he stopped short. He realized that these were the words he had really wanted to hear in coming to see the Pope in person.

There was no doubt that the Pope had truly forgiven the people who had attempted to kill him. Seeing that, Mr. Ceroni felt the disbelief and suspicion he had developed in his heart over many years falling away. He had been a devout Catholic earlier in life, but after becoming a policeman and dealing with many crimes, a deep cynicism had gripped his heart. The Catholic Church was not guiltless. Over time, he had lost his respect for the Catholic Church and had become distant from it. Yet that did not mean that he completely lost faith. He believed in the God that resided in himself; he just wasn't sure this was the same God that the Church taught about.

He did not know any intricate theology, yet he believed that Jesus was the Savior. However, he could never believe that "the Kingdom of God", which Jesus had mentioned in his early mission, was accomplished by Jesus' crucifixion and resurrection. He could not possibly be convinced by the view, as taught by the Church, that the work of salvation had been completed by Jesus' death and resurrection two thousand years ago. He had seen too much of the darker side of human nature—even among Christians—to believe that was enough.

However, since his interrogation of Father Yamamoto, he felt his faith in God and Jesus revive. The Revelation of the True Heart of Jesus acknowledged that the coming of the Kingdom of God on earth had been interrupted by Jesus' death. This made sense to him, and it interested him. He certainly did not think that the Kingdom of God had been realized on earth. The venerable Catholic Church herself was far from ideal, at least in his eyes. That was why the Revelation of the True Heart of Jesus gave him new hope. Discovering that Jesus' cross was not the final goal did not deny the value of Jesus or of Christianity but seemed to promise something more.

Mr. Ceroni made up his mind to accept the Pope's proposal not to file charges against the criminals.

The news of Pope Pax I's miraculous recovery spread worldwide. Sister Theresa pleaded that her name not be revealed publicly, and Pax I agreed to comply with her wish. He asked those who were present at the incident not to mention her to anyone. A statement issued by the acting Pope, Cardinal Toni, explained that the glory of God was fully revealed when people began to pray.

Sister Theresa wished to visit the St. Francis's town of Assisi, and the Pope immediately granted that Father Yamamoto and Father Schillebeeckx should accompany her there. The three of them visited a convent in Assisi, using an official car of the Vatican.

The miraculous recovery of Pax I brought a great joy not only to Catholics but also to many other people. Among all the gloomy, sorrowful incidents, atrocious crimes and wars in the world, Pax I's recovery was bright news that warmed people's hearts.

Ten days after his miraculous recovery of consciousness, the pontiff appeared, in good health, on the terrace before the eyes of the people gathered at St. Peter's Square and to the people all over the world. Father Yamamoto, Father Schillebeeckx, and Sister Theresa returned from Assisi and rushed to the Square.

"I am here again because of God's grace and because of your prayers, love, and support. I am very grateful to you. Please continue to pray. God has taught me through this incident how being united beyond differences in denominations and religions is wonderful and necessary," said Pope Pax I, waving to the people with a smile on his face.

The people gathered at the Square applauded thunderously. People all over the world were listening. The Pope continued to speak.

"Everyone, please do not forget why I was healed. It was because of God's grace and your prayers and also because of people honestly seeking the heart of Jesus. The important thing is not how I was miraculously healed but rather to seek the heart of Jesus. We must return to the point of seeking the heart of God and Jesus.

If you seek the heart of God and Jesus, a miracle may perhaps occur, and an illness may be healed, or various graces may be given. It is never the other way. Yet please yearn and search for the heart of Jesus in and of itself. Then Jesus will be with you. That is indeed the way which will lead humankind to a peaceful and happy world. Thank you all very much. May God abundantly bless you, your families, your countries, and your religions."

The next day, a Vatican personnel change was announced. A cardinal who had long been in the position of chairman of the Council for Interreligious Dialogue could no longer attend to his duties because of illness, and they had to appoint a new chairman. People were shocked and disappointed by Pax I's selection. Cardinal Domenico Cassini, who belonged to a highly conservative wing, was appointed.

Cardinal Cassini heard the murmur of surprise and disappointment at his appointment. As he listened, his heart ached, feeling how much he had been hurting the heart of God and Jesus and how much grief he had given them and other people by his hidebound ways. Yet, at the same time he had a very strange sensation. He noticed a refreshing feeling he had never experienced before arising from deep within his heart. This was something he had never expected. And in his mind, an incident that took place a few days before rose up again.

"Cardinal Cassini, I'm thinking of appointing you as the chairman of the Council for Interreligious Dialogue. Will you accept it?"

When Pope Pax I consulted him about the new appointment in advance, he was so surprised he couldn't believe his ears. Pax I was giving one of the most important responsibilities—a responsibility that would determine the future of the Catholic Church and the world—to the very person who had tried to kill him.

"I am not at all qualified for it. I was thinking of resigning as cardinal."

"No, Cardinal Cassini. This is not my desire. It is the desire of Jesus, because you can understand the significance and the value of the Revelation of the True Heart of Jesus more deeply than anyone else."

Cardinal Cassini was perplexed, unable to understand what that meant. However, as he recollected Pope's words, he was now able to feel that what he had said was true.

An indescribably fresh and sweet feeling welled up quietly from the bottom of his heart. It soon reached his entire body, and he felt it would overflow.

"I may have touched on the true love and true heart of Jesus."

As he said so to himself, he put his hand into his breast pocket inside his jacket to search for something. It was the pendant Sister Theresa had offered to Pax I, which the Holy Father had personally put around Cardinal Cassini's neck when he declared the new appointment. The rose petal which Jesus' tears had touched, which had healed Pax I was inside of it, maintaining its fresh brightness. Cardinal Cassini held the pendant in his hand for a long time, immersed in the bliss of the forgiven, and unconscious of the passage of time.

The End

ISBN-10: 1477683410
ISBN-13: 978-1477683415

Made in the USA
San Bernardino, CA
08 June 2016